LOSER

Sabra Benedict

Published by Porter Party Publishing 2017
porterpartypublishing@gmail.com

Book/Cover design by Sabra Benedict / Canva.com

This book is a work of fiction. Names, characters, places, and incidents either are products of the author's imagination or are used fictitiously. Any resemblance to actual persons, living or dead, events, or locales is entirely coincidental.

Printed in the United States of America

ISBN-10: 0-9988460-0-7
ISBN-13: 978-0-9988460-0-2

Dedicated to:

My family, immediate and extended, for the endless material.
   (If you're reading this, please keep speaking to me.)

My husband, for the endless support.

Solstice MFA in Creative Writing Program at Pine Manor College, for contributing to my growth as a writer.

Chapter 1

No mother expects to bury her daughter. And she was my favorite.

Our glasses made music when they clinked together. Nira, my oldest, and I were celebrating her raise. We sat in a fancy restaurant over bleached white linen tablecloths and intricately patterned silverware. It was nice to get out of the house.

Nira rubbed her stomach.

The crispy calamari and buttery baked stuffed lobster were delicious. "Eat too much?" I asked.

"Yes, but it was worth it. And I'm going to eat dessert, too."

I laughed.

Nira perused the drink menu. "With Sambuca," she added and sipped her champagne.

"Maybe we shouldn't order dessert. We won't look very good at the park." I enjoyed visiting various parks around Yonkers and New York City, often so I could lay out and bake under the sun.

"Like I care," Nira said, a small smirk on her face. She was far from being a fan of the outdoors. It was one of the few differences between us. The lack of sun damage to her skin made her appear younger than her thirty years. I was brown and leathery.

"I don't think I can afford dessert," I said. "Your father barely gave me any money."

"It's my treat." Nira was already prepared, always was.

I tried to smile, but Adam's stinginess gnawed at my stomach. "I should be taking you out, not the other way around."

Nira shrugged. "It's okay," she said. She finished her champagne as the waiter walked over to the table.

"Did you decide if you'd like dessert?" he asked. He was handsome. Earlier we joked about his good looks and what activities we'd like to perform on his naked body.

"I'll have the brownie sundae and she'll have the tiramisu," Nira said. "And we'll both have Sambuca." Her smile grew wider.

"Nira." I laughed as the waiter walked away.

"It's fine. So, how is Dad doing, anyway?"

Nira hadn't visited us in several weeks. "The same," I answered.

"Still on the couch, rotting?"

"Of course. He also missed the payment for the gym so I can't go right now." And I was trying so hard to feel good about myself, to ignore the lazy lump on the couch by killing time at the gym. "There's no money for groceries but he still manages to have a drink available whenever he wants one."

Nira sighed. "Yeah, yeah. If you don't like it then leave." Nira started the tough love routine several months earlier, having grown weary long ago of listening to me complain. I couldn't blame her. I was tired of hearing myself.

I let out a deep sigh that started in the pit of my stomach. I was always concentrating on my breathing, trying to stay strong. "I know. But what would I do? I haven't worked in decades."

The gorgeous waiter returned with our Sambuca and desserts.

We dug in. I looked across the table, as if in a mirror. Right hands wrapped around forks, left hands on our laps. I smiled.

Dessert was enjoyed in a slow, rhythmic manner while we relaxed in our chairs, gripping our glasses of Sambuca.

"Where's Peter tonight?" I asked. Peter was Nira's live-in boyfriend.

"He's home, probably playing his video games." Nira sipped her dessert drink and scrunched her face in disgust. "I don't know what I was thinking ordering this thing."

I giggled up wine. "I didn't want to say anything but I didn't think you'd like it."

"Funny, thanks," Nira said and laughed.

She settled the bill. I tried not to dwell on the fact that my daughter was forced to treat me to dinner. We walked out to the parking lot.

"Next week?" I asked. We hugged.

"I'll try. I'll let you know in a few days, okay?"

"Sure. Text me when you get home." I got into my car and drove off, a short two-minute drive from the restaurant.

Nira never texted me. She never arrived safely home. Instead, a drunk teenager drove through a busy intersection without tapping his brakes at the stop sign, rammed into the side of Nira's car, and caused her beautiful body to be splattered across the highway.

*

I could feel the warm sun on my cheeks, burning through my eyelids every time I closed my eyes. Maybe Nira was making the day of the funeral beautiful so that I wouldn't feel so terrible—like I was the dead one. I could almost forget where I was and imagine myself stretched across a bench at the park, sipping from a water bottle and getting a healthy dose of people watching.

Adam broke apart into little pieces. I didn't crack. Despite his bulk, I held him up throughout the service. At the cemetery, as friends and family shoveled fresh dirt on my daughter's coffin, Adam crumpled into a chair. He wasn't used to doing much more than sit anyway, aside from drinking. He did so much nothing and drank so much booze that his hips corroded and he only recently recovered from two hip replacement surgeries. He was sixty-one.

Sarah sobbed and leaned on Eric. They hadn't been close since sharing space in my womb twenty-three years earlier. His face was serious, but there were no tears. His hard-earned muscles pressed against his ironed suit, and he wore shiny loafers on what I was sure were manicured feet. Sarah was embarrassing in an old dress that looked like a potato sack on her shrinking body.

Standing there under the glaring sun and surrounded by my family, I was reminded of when we buried my middle sister Gabriella ten years earlier. No one expected that either. She overdosed on heroin after a boyfriend helped her become addicted and abandon everything in her life. I was the only one who acknowledged she was using, the only one who she hadn't driven away. The only one to witness her rotting. I couldn't get her to stop—not by threatening to out her or to report her to the police. Nothing. Days before she died, she asked me to snort the drug with her. I refused because of the love for my family. If only she'd loved something that much. At Gabriella's funeral, my mother threw herself on the coffin—more dramatic than in any movie I ever saw. That's what the death of your favorite child can do to you. Thank God she didn't know about the autopsy. We were never able to gather the courage to tell her that Gabriella had been cut open and dissected against our wishes, against our religion and faith, trapping her soul forever and forcing us to bury her with this lie that could never be rectified, never be corrected. This time, as they buried their granddaughter, my parents stayed seated, too old and shocked to stand.

When Nira was put to rest the family gathered to sit Shiva. Nira's apartment in downtown New York City was too small, so we gathered at my and Adam's house. We'd bought it when we were forced to downsize after Adam lost his popular board game manufacturing company because he'd invested with the wrong people and then suffered a stroke. We chose the town I grew up in—Yonkers, New York. Deciding where to settle down was easy. I wanted to be near my parents since none of us were getting any younger and Adam had no family to move close to. He grew up tortured and alone in the New York City foster care system. He hadn't formed a single relationship to maintain. We chose a 1,400 square foot home in need of TLC, which we would never give. Our house was a cubic zirconia among diamonds. The dull yellow grass and peeling paint drew the angry eye of every neighbor. We brought down their home values.

Elsa, my youngest sister, brought pies and chocolate chip meringues. I would have preferred real food. Or maybe the potato chips I loved so much that I wore them on my flabby butt, muffin top, and floppy arms. I thought Elsa should've known better, would've wanted something healthy to satisfy the organic kick that made her so skinny.

"I brought Nira's favorites," she said before I could ask.

Our family was small—eight of us sat in the living room on a circular velvet couch. It was Nira's favorite room, oversized with pastel wallpaper, a portable fireplace, and flat screen television. Whenever Nira came to visit, she made me promise to make it clear to Adam that the girls would be hanging out in that room. Now the characters that made up my family sat before me. And all I wanted to do was catch Nira's eye so we could laugh together and figure out a quick getaway. God, how I needed a drink.

*

When the doorbell rang I was picking at my cuticles. I was so captivated by pulling the white skin off my nail that it rang twice before I forced myself to move from the couch. I even managed to absorb myself so deeply that I blocked out the barking of our elderly dogs, Maxie the overweight Shih Tzu and Mo the skeletal Maltese. Poor things were being ignored a lot since I was self-absorbed in pity.

Peter stood outside. I hadn't seen him since the funeral two weeks earlier.

I scratched at the dry patch of skin on my arm, near the elbow, before pulling open the screen door. He and Nira had lived twenty minutes away. He'd never dropped by without a reason before. "You could've just come inside."

He shook his head and hesitated as I stepped aside to let him in. "I don't think so," he said after an unusual awkward silence, feet still rooted on the concrete stair.

I stepped outside and let the door slam behind me. The dogs watched us, confused with Peter's non-greeting. Usually when Peter came over it was playtime. He was even more frail than usual. Delicate. "You don't want to come in?"

"I can't." He looked past me and into the house, and then winced as if in pain. "That's not why I'm here," he said and handed me an envelope.

"What is this?" I asked.

"Nira's will. She put it together a few months ago. She suggested I do the same but I never got around to it."

I was surprised at Nira. While she was responsible, she'd never mentioned anything about a will. I swallowed the rapidly growing lump in my throat. "Where'd you find it?" I asked. I'd already visited their apartment and boxed up most of Nira's things.

"She gave it to me for safekeeping. I'd forgotten, but it was in one of my game cases."

I imagined that Peter wasn't doing much more than playing those video games. Although to be fair, he was a professional video game tester. "Well, thanks for bringing it over. You sure you won't come in?"

Maxie barked right then, as if also inviting Peter inside.

"I can't," was all he said before turning around and walking away.

I waited a minute, hoping he'd come back. No such luck. From what I knew of Peter, he was never one to confront his problems. He was a happy-go-lucky guy that let everything roll right off his shoulders. Except for this, naturally.

When I gave Adam the will he called his lawyer to set up a meeting. We invited Peter to attend. I ached for his company, for the laugh that always put a smile on Nira's face. But I guess he just couldn't bring himself to come.

*

We were in downtown New York City waiting to find out what Nira's will said. A letter with the will dictated that we gather with a lawyer and that all four of us be there. It isn't typical anymore to meet in an attorney's office to discuss a will. More often than not the will is distributed to the executor and beneficiaries and that's the end. I think Nira wanted it done this way because we'd need a mediator. She wasn't wrong.

Adam and our two remaining children dragged their feet into the bright office—two huge windows allowed an abundance of light to stream in. I hesitated in the doorway. The hot blood pumped to my cheeks and the sticky sweat collected on my forehead. The last available chair rested in the corner of the oversized room. I settled there alone. The chair was hard and uncomfortable; it reminded me of the chairs in my parents' home, a home filled with furniture as stiff as the people. My feet dangled, not quite touching the ground. I watched my only living daughter play with her dirty fingernails, my son stare at his feet, my husband clench his jaw. We waited to find out how we could benefit from our loved one's death.

"Where is this guy?" Sarah said. She squirmed in her seat. "Why do I even have to be here?"

Eric stared at her and gave her a look we all knew too well, a look of ice that couldn't be broken by a sharp pick. Even his thick glasses did nothing to dull the intensity throbbing from his eyes. "Don't be a bitch," he said in a soft, even voice. "It isn't about you. For once." It was almost nice that he spoke up for Nira, but it had to be more about attacking Sarah. As much as I loved Eric, I couldn't say he felt the same for the rest of us. When he spoke at family gatherings it was to put one of us down. On rare occasions he would crack a joke. That was the Eric I enjoyed most, but I didn't get to see him often.

Adam stood up and walked to the doorway. He filled up the entire space of the doorframe and glared at our children. "Both of you need to shut up." Elegant as always. I knew that he hurt inside, that he loved and missed Nira in his own way. And that he would take his hurt out on the rest of us.

Thomas Sinclair, Adam's lawyer, walked into the room. The three of us had met in Albany where they played on the SUNY wrestling team.

Thomas still maintained his muscular, booming physique. After Adam separated his shoulder and wrestled against the doctor's orders, he never regained full use of his arm. The rest of him then softened and widened.

Sarah opened her mouth to say something smart. She said many times she knew she wouldn't be in the will and didn't want to come along since her relationship with Nira was almost non-existent. Nira brought me constant joy. I was always proud of her. But Sarah... she was a bottomless well of disappointment and could never get past my deep appreciation for Nira. Eric wasn't sure his attendance was necessary, either, as he'd always been closer to Sarah than Nira, but I suspected he felt it necessary to take on Nira's role of family mediator and caretaker. It was hard for both twins to be there. They would've rather been mourning in solitude than with the family, to have been locked away in a dark room, drowning in a sea of secret tears.

"Hello Browns," Thomas said. He surveyed the room while providing a manly pat to Adam's back, and then tossed his shiny black suitcase onto the desk next to a mug featuring a Great Dane, the mascot for SUNY.

"How you holding up?" Thomas asked Adam in a low tone, as if the rest of us weren't in the room.

Adam made some reference to wrestling that I didn't understand. Thomas thought it was hilarious. I used to shake with laughter because of Adam, too. Sometimes I still did, when I couldn't help myself, when I forgot how bitter I was. But more often, I shook from anger.

Both men were seated. "I guess we'll just get this over with?" Thomas asked.

We'd worked with Thomas for a long time. There wasn't much he didn't know about our family, but he was Adam's lawyer before anyone else's. I'd contacted him once, years ago, about divorcing Adam. Thomas couldn't understand why. Adam's the life of the party, he claimed. Yes, but what happened when the party stopped? When the children needed to be raised, colleges chosen? Adam was an additional child. It was exhausting.

"Can we?" I asked, speaking for the first time in hours. I woke up a mute and fully embraced it when everyone stopped bothering me with "Mom's" and "Janie's". Now the words ripped at my throat.

Thomas nodded and pulled a document from his briefcase. The will. Nira's will. My eyes blurred. I didn't want to be in the room anymore. It started to close in on me. I'd thought it was so big before. Now it crushed me. I took one deep breath and then another.

"Mom?" Sarah drew attention to me and everyone looked.

I offered a weak smile and tried to wink at her. I probably looked like I was having a stroke.

"You okay?" she asked.

"Do you need to step outside?" Thomas offered.

Adam shook his head. "We said we wanted to get this over with."

I ignored him and nodded at Thomas. "Just continue." I didn't want anything prolonging this moment.

Thomas snorted—a side effect of getting elbowed in the nose one too many times during wrestling. "It's not very long." He made eye contact with Adam before taking the plunge. "Movie and book collection to be evenly distributed between my brother Eric Brown and my partner Peter MacDonald. Jewelry to my sister Sarah Brown," he said.

I caught Sarah's eye and flooded with warmth, grateful that Nira included her. It was painful when they stopped having a relationship while Nira was alive—to think that there might be hatred in death was too much.

Thomas kept talking. "Anything else that's discovered of value is to be distributed at the discretion of my mother, Janie Brown."

"What? Janie?" Adam asked. His face was red. Sometimes the children still called him tomato head when he grew angry. He sat on the edge of his chair, beads of sweat forming on his forehead. "Why Janie?"

Thomas glanced at me. I looked away. "Because that's the way Nira wanted it, Adam," he said.

"This is bullshit."

"Dad," Eric said and shook his head. "Not now."

Adam stopped talking, but didn't lean back in his chair. He was so good at making bad things worse.

Sarah was crying in silence. I almost didn't notice the plump tears rolling down her gaunt cheeks. I didn't think she'd stop losing weight. My baby. I stood and went to her. Too heavy with grief to kneel, I wiped the tears from her face and placed a hand on her shoulder. The tears were flowing from my own eyes now. The first tears I'd shed since that awful day. Using the hand that wasn't on Sarah's shoulder I wiped away the puddles that formed under my eyes.

"Fine, fine. Is there more?" Adam asked.

Sarah rolled her eyes at Adam and I tightened my grip on her shoulder. The less aggravated he was the quicker this would be over.

"Nira had life insurance through her job," Thomas said. "The amount was matched by them when she passed." He paused. If the action was for dramatic effect, he was successful. "It's all been left to Janie."

Eric spoke first—which was a first in itself. "How much? Mom, you can invest," he said. He tried to smile. He worked at a tax firm in Boston. His job, and more specifically money, was one of the few things he got excited about.

Adam's eyes were about to pop from his skull. "Janie is in charge of distributing the money?"

Thomas shook his head. "Nira didn't mean for the money to be left for distribution." He looked at Eric. "There's slightly over half a million in a private trust account for Janie."

"You've got to be joking," Adam said and laughed. It sounded more like a noise an animal would make. Hee-haw.

"That's everything," Thomas said. "Janie, if you want to stay we can discuss Nira's wishes."

Sarah and Eric stood at the same time. "Let's get out of here," Sarah whined.

Adam shook his head. "This is un-fucking-believable. After everything I did for Nira... she couldn't have left me something?"

"That's probably why she didn't leave you anything, your fucked up attitude," Eric said.

Thomas cleared his throat. No one paid him any attention.

"Ass," Sarah said to Adam.

He glanced at Thomas before turning back to Sarah. "Watch your fucking language."

"We're leaving." Eric's beefy arm pulled at his sister's tiny wrist as he dragged her from the room. They'd driven in from Boston, where Sarah also lived, and wanted to hurry back in order to avoid rush hour traffic. Adam and I offered to let them stay at our house, but neither child took us up on it. No one enjoyed coming to our home. Why would they? It was so stifling even I couldn't bear it.

I refused to look at Adam. I didn't know what Nira was thinking, but I didn't deserve Adam's wrath.

He huffed and puffed.

"Okay, Adam. What do you want from me?" Thomas asked. "This is her last will and testament."

"I want to see it."

"Would I lie to you?"

I stood up. I'd heard enough.

"What are you doing?" Adam said.

"I don't need to sit here and listen to you argue with Thomas."

Adam stood, too. "Wait. Don't you dare leave."

"Why not? What's done is done." It wasn't often that I stood up to Adam but I needed to get out of that office. I needed fresh air like a mosquito needed blood.

I turned to Thomas, who was seated on the edge of his seat ready to flee. "Thomas, why don't you talk to Adam? I'll call you tomorrow." I'd pay for that later.

Outside I took a deep breath of air and allowed myself to smile. It was as if Nira still needed to have the final word. And this time it was a good one.

Chapter 2

I collapsed into the driver's seat of my silver station wagon. The car was more a faded gray now than silver, the tan leather seats browned and torn. Adam's brand new mustang convertible, red, of course, was parked on the opposite side of the lot because I refused to ride in the same car as him. I plopped my head back against the seat rest. What the hell was Nira thinking? The gesture... it was thoughtful like her, and I appreciated it, but she knew better. That money was going to force a confrontation with Adam—the very thing I tried to avoid day in and day out. It was much better when we didn't speak. Now he would want to talk—well, to yell, since in the thirty-two years we'd been married he'd never spoken at a normal volume. It was so tempting to just hand the money over. But that's not what Nira wanted. It was bad enough that I now had to cope without her, but a new fight with Adam? I had no energy for that. I had no fight left. The loss of Nira, the never-ending awfulness of Adam—the stress might kill me. What the hell was I going to do? Maybe it was time I just walked away.

I put the key in the ignition and turned the engine over. Running my hand up and down the steering wheel I remembered the first time we bought a station wagon. Nira was three years old. It protected us. In the past, a safe car was one of the few things Adam allowed me to own. Every time I needed a new one he bought me the upgraded version of the one I loved. I pulled out of the spot and drove home. I should have begged Adam to buy one for Nira.

I arrived at the house first. In all likelihood Adam was still throwing a tantrum at the lawyer's office. The dogs hopped around in excitement at having their favorite human companion back. I greeted them with soft pats on the head and sat down in Adam's living room. He and I no longer shared it. Around five years earlier, I'd turned the second bedroom into my own living room with a daybed. When I wasn't in the kitchen or laundry room I was there, relaxing in my own space. Adam kept the living room and master bedroom suite with its king-size bed.

I cuddled with the dogs for a few minutes. Maxie's fur was always comforting—it was soft and smooth, like an expensive teddy bear's. The warmth from Mo's small body wasn't bad, either.

I felt Adam's presence before he entered the house. He pushed open the door and his footsteps shook the floor, worse than usual. The dogs ran behind the television console. I thought of the small overnight bag I kept in the trunk of my car. I was never sure when or where I'd run off to, but needed to be prepared.

Adam's entrance was beyond dramatic. The storm door was already hanging on by a single hinge due to his lack of pride in our home. As it crashed into the doorframe a crack spread across the width of the glass.

He glared at me, the nastiest look he could muster. Nira called it his "shit-eating face."

"You disgust me," he roared. King of the jungle.

I was grateful that the dogs were already hiding, because their ears would've hurt from the rough pitch of his voice. Mine did. I wished I'd headed right upstairs to my room when I first got home. I should've known better.

"I can understand you're frustrated, but don't take it out on me," I replied, my mantra.

Adam didn't sit down. He paced. It was more exercise than I'd seen him do in the past twenty years. His chicken legs carried him back and forth across the room, his beer gut wobbling in beat with his double chin.

"You knew about this." He stood before me, leaning into my face.

"No, I didn't." He was a little too close. I could smell his rotten teeth.

"I find that hard to believe. You're telling me Nira never mentioned this to you?"

"She never mentioned it." So many of our conversations were based in repetition.

"You're a liar," Adam spat. "A dirty fucking liar. You probably plotted with Nira. Now what? What are you going to do with that money? No one is going to want you. That money won't make you attractive."

I shook my head and tried to stand without bumping into him, but his large frame blocked me so I dropped back into the seat.

"Where do you think you're going?"

"Well, I'm not going to sit here and be screamed at."

"You'll stay. And I'm not screaming. This is how I talk."

I sat still, frozen. No words came to me.

Adam clenched and unclenched his fists. "Say something."

"What do you want me to say, Adam?"

"That you know Nira did this to spite me."

"I'm not going to say that because it isn't true. Why would Nira do that?" I hated that I was the constant voice of reason, that Adam could never be realistic or logical on his own.

"You're an idiot. She always loved you more," he said. He paused to spew more hatred with his eyes, and then walked into the kitchen. "Did you pick me up some more vodka? I need a shot."

"No, I didn't." Since he was no longer blocking me I was free to escape. But I stayed seated. Lifeless.

"What the fuck, Janie?" He stormed back into the living room. "What did you do with the fifty bucks I gave you?"

"I got my prescription." The one I always had to fight for the money to refill. The one that was supposed to keep me sane, or as sane as possible in my current miserable predicament. The pills were meant to treat my anxiety but really made living with Adam a whole lot easier. One would think he'd appreciate that and give me the money to refill the medication.

"Jesus," he said.

I tasted his disgust.

"You don't think I believe that, do you? You had a date with one of your lovers," he said. He sounded so sure of himself I almost believed the lie. I never once cheated on Adam and yet he "knew" I did whenever the chance arose. Years of trying to convince him that I've never even looked at another man had been fruitless.

I shook my head, unable to muster the words to defend myself for a crime I didn't commit.

Adam sank into the couch. He twisted his heavy body and reached in his back pocket, pulling out his wallet, already forgetting his last accusation toward me. "I'll give you twenty bucks to grab me some vodka and whatever you want for yourself."

"Twenty dollars?"

"When you get into Nira's trust you can buy me all the vodka you want." He laughed. I'm sure he thought I would.

I took the money, grabbed my purse, and dashed out of the house. Nira's life insurance wasn't going to be spent on alcohol for Adam. If I was going to take my dead daughter's money it was going to be used on something she would've wanted. On me being happy. I could go to school. Or take singing lessons again. Join a choir. Adam forbade all that long ago when we'd stopped being a team. For a while there I'd been allowed a voice.

*

I was thirty years old when I became pregnant with Nira. Adam had received a promotion a few years earlier from the paper store where he worked while I finished college. The promotion included a transfer to Boston so we moved into a one-bedroom apartment downtown. He loved living in the city, but I was ready to move into a real house, a place we could call home.

"I think we should consider Weston," I said and pointed to the map stretched out on the worn kitchen table before us.

Adam tilted his head to the side and rubbed his chin. "Maybe. I did hear they have a good public school district."

I laughed. "We don't want our kid being a dummy, huh?"

He grinned. "They have good athletics, too."

"Sounds well-rounded." I tried to wiggle away before he could tickle me in the ribs. "I actually checked the help wanted section and they have a lot of teaching positions. I don't think I'll have a problem finding something after the baby is born."

"Okay, so it's definitely a place for us to think seriously about."

I nodded and rubbed my stomach. "If we can afford it."

"I've always wanted to live in a nice, wealthy neighborhood." He nodded. "We can afford it."

"Just wanted to make sure you agreed," I said.

Adam leaned forward and kissed me on the forehead. "Agreed." He pushed the chair away from the table and stood. "Let's take a break from this for a little bit?" I nodded and he headed over to the refrigerator. "Are you hungry?"

"Whatcha got?"

He smiled and his mustache crinkled under his nose. "I made eggplant parmesan."

"You did? When?"

"When you went to visit your mother. You were gone forever." Adam pulled a large Tupperware container from the second refrigerator shelf.

I'd returned that morning from an overnight stay back in Yonkers, a seven-hour round-trip drive from Boston, to tell my parents I was pregnant. Since they were so stoic it was often better to have discussions face to face, where I could observe both voice and action, rather than limiting myself to tone over the phone. I don't know why, it made no difference. I still didn't know if they were happy about my pregnancy or not.

"I missed you, too," I said and stood, removing a loaf of Italian bread from the shiny silver engraved breadbox my grandmother gave us for our wedding. "I'll make garlic bread." I squeezed by Adam and grabbed margarine, garlic butter, and minced garlic from the refrigerator.

"Sounds good. I just want to stick this in the oven to heat it up for a bit." He turned the knob to preheat the oven to a low setting and put the cheese-coated eggplant in while I slathered the bread. I placed the loaf on a shelf before closing the oven door. It was a small oven, apartment-sized, and perfecting its use took us awhile.

We were a good team. We were equals. I never thought I could love someone so much.

"How much time do we have?" He said, wrapping his arms around me and pulling me in for a soft kiss. I closed my eyes and kissed him back, enjoying the subtle scent of his aftershave.

When we pulled apart I glanced at the clock above the stove. "Twenty minutes?" The words were barely out of my mouth when he began grazing the skin of my neck and shoulders with butterfly kisses. Giggling, I pushed him away and looked down at my still flat stomach.

Adam placed his hand on my belly. "You think she'll be okay?"

"She?"

He nodded.

"She'll be fine."

Hands clasped together, we headed down the dim hallway to our cramped bedroom.

We bought a house in Weston. I stayed home, birthed child after child, and depended on Adam for my financial well-being. He made a lot of money over the years, before selling part of the company and having the stroke. All this while I continued to stay at home, beginning to rot away.

*

I tried to clear my head while I drove by drowning out my thoughts with headache inducing music. I went to the liquor store with Adam's twenty dollars, walked right inside and down the vodka aisle. Then realized the ridiculousness of what I was doing. If I did this I lost. I would be a loser. Hopeless and helpless and plain pathetic. So I turned around and went to stay with Elsa, who also lived in Yonkers. She shared a 6 bedroom Victorian with Billy, her award winning dancer boyfriend of seven years and the one man she'd seriously dated after her husband cheated with, and gave her jewelry away to, several strippers at the Pussycat Lounge. Elsa had been with her husband since she was thirteen and the day he broke her heart I wanted to hunt him down and break his face. At least she was able to keep the enormous house. I have a much better relationship with Billy. Although I didn't sing in front of people anymore, Billy always managed to coerce me into performing some type of ballad that he could dance to. We made an entertaining pair and nothing beat the pride that emanated from my sister.

Elsa was more excited about the money than I was. She had ideas about where I should go, what I should do. Who I should take with me. Ideas of grandeur that didn't appeal to me. My goals were much simpler: Be happy and alone.

"That's pretty amazing of Nira," Elsa said and walked into the living room holding a bowl of popcorn. The first batch she made was a disaster. The stench of burnt popcorn still lingered inside my nostrils.

I was seated on Elsa's black leather couch—which I hated. It was always sticking to me, to the back of my fat thighs. I'm sure it never bothered Elsa, the petite bitch. She made a point of telling people how tiny she was, as if they couldn't see it with their own two eyes. She sat next to me and offered the bowl. I shook my head and continued to grip my wine glass.

"What?" She drowned her hand in the popcorn.

"I'm not hungry." I'm grieving. Normally I was the type of person who, when depressed, ate. But now the despair was filling up my stomach. I'd still been hungry at first, still craved salty foods. Then, one day, my appetite vanished. I think it was when I realized I really truly couldn't flee to Nira and Peter's for the night anymore. I wouldn't hear from Nira every day at 3:30 PM when she got out of work and wanted to share stories of the kindergartners she taught.

And I was having trouble accepting having walked out. I didn't want to go back. Did I have to? Could I just leave Adam? We'd spent so many years together I didn't know if we could be apart. Independent. But I did know that if I went back I'd continue to be miserable.

"Wait," Elsa said, breaking me from my trance. "You wouldn't eat the salmon and now you won't eat popcorn? You'll never pull off the anorexic look."

A stranger wouldn't know whether she was kidding or not. "Afraid you won't be the tiny one anymore, sis?"

We laughed, like women who never lost a sister, a daughter, or a niece. I stuck my hand in the popcorn, after all.

"How long do you want to stay?" Elsa spit out kernels when she talked.

"A few days?" Forever?

"Sure. Billy won't be back until the weekend. But you should find your own lawyer ASAP."

"Do you have a lawyer to recommend?"

She picked a piece of corn from between her teeth. I loved how she reserved that side of her for me. "Talk to Rick, he's a lawyer."

"My ex-boyfriend Rick?"

Elsa rolled her eyes. She had every right to.

For a second, I felt like the shy girl I'd been in high school. But the exhaustion that rendered me weak for so many years now made me feel that it didn't matter what happened. It all ended the same way—we'd all die someday. "What's his number?"

"Really? You'll really call him?"

I could feel a smirk sneak up on my lips at her doubt. "Yes, I'll call him." I put my wine glass on the coffee table. "I'll call him right now. Give me the number."

Elsa eyed the clock, which revealed the time as past 8:00 PM. "You'll end up getting his answering machine now."

"Just give me the number," I said and took the phone from its cradle on the end table.

She did a quick Internet search and read me the number from her cell phone.

The phone rang twice before he answered. "Wilson's Law," he announced.

"Hi, Rick? This is Janie. Janie Freedman." I'd decided to go back to my maiden name, although both names were cursed. It wouldn't be legal until the divorce was final, but at least I could pretend.

"Janie?" Oh my God, he sounded the same. Did I?

"Yes."

"Hi! I can't believe it's you!"

"Me neither," I said, laughing.

"What can I do for you?"

I glanced at Elsa. She was staring at me, her mouth and eyes open wide. "I have a few legal questions."

"Sure. Why don't you come in for an appointment? Do you want to come in tomorrow? I could see you at 1:00 PM." He sounded so eager to help. It felt familiar and strange at the same time.

"Okay." My mouth only allowed one word to come out.

"Good. My office is located at 1 Penn Plaza. Enter the lobby and take the elevator to the 4th floor. Walk through the glass doors to 'Wilson's Law' and check in with the receptionist."

"Sounds great. I'll see you tomorrow. Thanks." I hung up the phone.

Elsa applauded.

I bowed.

Chapter 3

I wished I'd brought someone to Rick's office with me. So much time had passed since we last saw one another that I felt like I was meeting a stranger.

A tiny blonde woman with a high-pitched voice greeted me when I walked into the office. She looked exactly how I remembered Rick's type to be. She was seated behind a mahogany desk painting her nails a deep blue and wore enough makeup to outfit several fashion models. I wondered how Rick could stand to look at her without laughing. She resembled a drunken clown. "Wilson's Law," she chirped.

Of course I just wanted to run. "Hi. I'm here to see Rick Wilson?" I'm not sure why it came out as a question.

She squinted her eyes and looked at something on the computer screen. "Who did you say you were?"

"Janie Br—er—Janie Freedman."

"I don't see you on the schedule, so I'll have to check with him." She stood. "Will he know what this is regarding?"

"I'm an old friend." Was I? This already felt awkward.

"Mmmhmm." She sounded as if she didn't believe me. "Please wait here." She wobbled away on heels too high, blowing air at her nails to dry them.

I tapped my foot to the beat of the music leaking from the speakers overhead. I was distracted, almost humming along, when one of Nira's favorite songs came on. The song was about a young woman who went after her dream and failed. Before I could work myself into tears the blonde secretary returned.

"Follow me." She gave a weak gesture and hobbled along.

I stayed behind her until she stopped short and we almost collided. She waved her hand forward and I slipped into Rick's office.

Rick appeared the same. Almost as if he hadn't aged, yet not plastic looking. He glided over to greet me with familiar ease. A quick kiss on the cheek almost had me swaying in his arms. He gently ushered me into a seat and sat behind his desk.

"You look great," he said.

He was either lying or blind. As the years passed my waist expanded and the bags under my eyes continued to grow darker and deeper. Rick was always an excellent kiss up.

"Thanks, you don't look so bad yourself. I was surprised you answered the phone so late last night."

"Oh, yeah, well, I don't have much going on at home at the moment."

I stared at him, confused.

"Margaret and I. We recently divorced."

"Oh, sorry to hear that." I wasn't. And there was no way he believed that I was.

"Thanks. It was about time."

"Really?" I tried to hide the shock from my voice. Rick had always been so successful at putting up a front that I'd assumed his marriage was a happy one.

Rick smiled. "It wasn't anything dramatic. No affair or anything. We just grew apart."

"Oh," I said and nodded. "I understand that."

"How're you?"

"I'm fine." I lied. I didn't know yet if we were the type of old friends that picked up where we left off, able to confide in one another.

"You don't have to lie to me, Janie," he said.

The blood rushed to my face. My rosy cheeks always gave me away.

Rick laughed. "You're still cute."

The blush deepened from red to purple.

"Things could be better," I admitted and scratched at my arm.

"I heard about Nira. I'm so sorry."

"I'm dealing with it the best I can."

"How are your parents?" He leaned back in his chair and crossed his legs. God he was sexy.

"Mom is well. Dad was diagnosed with Alzheimer's a while back, after Gabriella's death." Rick was out of town when my sister passed away. My family received a colorful crystal vase of flowers and a card with his condolences. Gabriella tried to sleep with him once. Elsa believed she succeeded.

"I'm sorry I couldn't be there for you then."

"It's okay." It wasn't. Adam took Gabriella's death hard because she was like a sister to him. I needed to be taken care of and he was inconsolable. Part of me believed that Rick stayed away during that time to avoid any drama. Although I never forgot about the possibility that my boyfriend had slept with my sister, I also wouldn't have caused a scene at my own sister's funeral.

"So, what's up? What do you need my help with?"

I tried to go into professional mode, a mode I hadn't enrolled in since before Nira was born. "Nira left all of her life insurance to me. Half a million."

"Well, that's great news! Are you and Adam going on a trip?"

Now, that was funny. "No, Nira left it to me."

"Just you? What about Adam?"

"He's less than thrilled. I said I understood growing apart from your wife because the same thing has happened to Adam and me. And now I'm stuck. Thomas, Adam's lawyer, presented the will because Nira didn't have a lawyer and I don't feel entirely comfortable working with him since he's really Adam's lawyer." I paused for breath. "Is there any way, I mean, I'm sure you're busy, but do you have a little time you could throw my way?"

"C'mon, Janie, you know the answer to that."

I'd hoped I did. "I owe you one."

"Just give me the lawyer's contact info."

I pulled a slip of paper from my purse and rattled off the information that I had for Thomas.

"Piece of cake," Rick said. "Do you know how this money was left to you?"

"It's in a trust account."

"Okay. I'd like you to check on the restrictions of the account and then call me with that information. I'll take care of the other lawyer and make sure everything is all set for you."

"I can do that. Thank you so much."

"Of course. Now that you owe me one, I think we should go grab a drink sometime soon," Rick said. I swear he winked at me.

I tried to laugh, but I was uncomfortable, and my throat was closing, so my laughter got trapped and instead I sounded like a donkey. I had only just told Rick my marriage was failing and he already wanted to get a drink? I would definitely need some time to process this. "Yes, sure. I'll call you after I get the trust information."

"Great. You take care, Janie. And don't be a freaking stranger." When he smiled a little dimple formed under his right cheek. I remembered that dimple. Too well.

*

Billy would be returning home soon. I was heavy with gassy nausea about returning to Adam. He was calling often, leaving bi-polar messages filled with tears and anger. I should have been home, consoling him; the dogs missed me; he missed me; there were no groceries left; how dare I leave him at a time like this; I must be out having an affair. And on and on until I could hear his voice ringing in my head long after I powered off the phone.

I took Rick's advice and headed to the trust company to check on the account. I felt like a wingless bird desperate for the air of independence. I supposed I could've just called, but it felt more important, more real, for me to go in person. Outside the decaying brick building I paused, took a deep breath of fresh air, and walked inside. There was a small seating area to my right, but no one there to greet me.

A small balding woman jerked her head around the corner of a cubicle. "Did you need help with something, dear?"

I did, but she didn't look like she'd be too helpful. Her bottle cap thick glasses made me wonder if she could see at all. "Is there a manager available?" I asked.

She disappeared behind the cubicle wall and then a different woman came around and greeted me.

"Hello, I'm Danielle. What can I help you with?" Danielle was slim and tidy in a pressed skirt-suit with her hair pinned back into a tight bun. She looked much more reliable than the little balding, blind woman and was young, maybe around Nira's age. But unlike Nira, she was vibrant and alive. Danielle offered a strong handshake.

"I'm here to find out the details of my account."

"Wonderful. Alice can actually help you," she said and took a step back as if to grab the woman from earlier.

"Wait," I said, forgetting to hesitate before opening my mouth— which was a new feeling. "I'm sorry. Would you assist me? I'd feel better if a manager was helping me out." I hoped that didn't seem rude.

Danielle nodded and a perfectly placed piece of hair fell into her eye. She blew upward to move it out of her face. "Of course. Come with me," she said and walked around the side of the ugly cubicle. I followed. We passed multiple cubes until we reached a back wall with a door. She pushed the door open and I stepped into a large, airy room without much furniture.

Within minutes we were seated and I was handing over my license, social security card, and Nira's death certificate. My hand shook as I slid everything across the table.

"What can I help you with today?" Danielle pecked away at the keyboard.

"I'd like to check on the restrictions for the account." I must've sounded unsure because Danielle stopped typing and relaxed in her seat.

"Is this your first time here?" Her voice was soothing, seamless.

"Yes," I said and nodded. I was nervous but couldn't stop smiling. Others might think this was a small accomplishment, but I was pretty excited. And I didn't get excited about much. Not anymore.

Danielle continued entering information into the computer while I fiddled with my purse strap. She stopped and pushed her chair back from the desk. "Let me just grab some paperwork from the printer in the hall." She was back before I could blink, placing a piece of paper and a pen in front of me. "Please look those over and sign at the X while I pull up the information you're interested in. The forms just include basic information about your account and your signature confirms you have read everything."

I nodded and looked at the paper in front of me. There was my name and address and account information. It was a little startling to see my name there, with money reflected in a positive amount. I was so used to seeing statements with negative balances or letters from collection agencies.

"I see why you were interested. This restriction is a little unusual," she said.

"Unusual?" I repeated.

"It's rather serious. All actions must be committed by you and you only and they must be completed in person," she informed me.

God, I loved Nira. I couldn't believe she had looked out for me like this, like how a mother looked out for her daughter. I know she loved Adam. But I guess she loved the thought of a happy mother more. Maybe she was tired of knowing her mother had to beg for money.

"That's great. To clarify—my husband can't access the account?"

Danielle offered a small smile, a smirk. "Correct," she said. "You are the sole beneficiary."

"Can I be alerted if someone else does try to access the account?"

"Certainly," Danielle said and turned back to the computer. "How would you like to be alerted?"

"By phone?"

"Not a problem."

We sat in silence for a few minutes while she worked her technological magic. Rather than fiddle my thumbs I scratched at my arm.

"Done," Danielle said and pushed her chair away from the desk. "Is there anything else I can help you with?"

"Is it possible for my lawyer to have access to the account?"

"Will he be helping to manage it?" Danielle asked.

"Possibly for a short while," I admitted.

"I can put his name down so he can access some information, but he won't be able to touch the funds."

"Okay, that sounds reasonable. His name is Richard Wilson." I provided her with his address and phone number.

Danielle pulled her chair back up to the keyboard and typed away. "Anything else?"

"No, thank you," I said. We both stood. I received another sturdy handshake.

"Please call if you need anything." She handed me a card.

"Okay. Thank you," I said again. I turned from her and hurried down the row of cubicles.

When I stepped outside and the sun hit my face I felt different. More alive. I quickly called Rick and filled him in on the trust account details. He let me know Thomas was made aware that I no longer needed his legal assistance.

Warmth flooded my face as I realized the opportunities before me. It was overwhelming. I could start a new life. I could go out and earn my own money and add it to the money my amazing daughter had left me. The reality of the things Adam didn't let me do or enjoy hit me harder every day.

Chapter 4

I let another week pass before I returned home to Adam and the dogs. It's not that I thought I was overstaying my welcome at Elsa's, but I missed my own space. I'd spent a lot of time making the spare bedroom the perfect hideaway for me and the dogs. Being at Elsa's just wasn't the same.

I pulled the station wagon into my spot in the garage, grabbed my bag from the back seat and walked up to the front door. I wanted to get this over with as quickly as possible. The dogs were barking before I'd even pulled open the door. I stepped inside. The house smelled musty, like old man. There was a pile of what I assumed to be dirty clothes and a couple bags of trash at the top of the basement stairs. The mirrors were still covered with sheets, indicating our need to not be vain during the time of a loved one's death. What a joke. The days when Adam cleaned up after himself and appreciated me were long gone.

Adam sat in his usual seat, the smooth brown leather reclining chair. He sat there so often that there was a grease spot where his head rested. When I walked into the living room and he turned to look at me he didn't lift his head, didn't offer a hand to help. Nothing unusual. I dropped my bag on the floor.

"You're back," he stated.

The dogs barked at my feet, relieved to be free of Adam. I knelt down and rubbed them on their soft little heads. I wondered if they would notice when Nira didn't come by anymore. They'd been saddened when Gabriella passed. She'd been the one to go with me when I adopted them and when Adam went on business trips she would come and stay with us.

I stood and caught Adam watching me.

"What?" I asked.

"What's for dinner?"

"Really?"

"Yes, really. With how long you've been gone I'd at least expect you to have some fucking dinner for me."

"I don't." I was shocked. How could he expect me to walk back in and start waiting on him again? Because I always did it before. No more.

"You don't." He shook his head and stared at the television.

I couldn't decide if he was going to get up or not and I wasn't waiting to find out. He'd always been more bark than bite, but I wasn't risking it. I picked up my bag and hurried up the stairs to my room, both dogs a few steps behind. I closed the door after them and sat on the bed. I didn't realize I was crying until I couldn't see through the tears. Once the well opened it was all over.

*

Adam was desperate for the money. He wouldn't let it go, tried to be sneaky on an amateur level, and was caught. He forged my name on paperwork he believed would allow him access to the trust. Too bad for him, Danielle at the trust company called to warn me.

I swallowed an anxiety pill with a glass of water and thought about how to pass the time before Adam returned home. He would no doubt be doing anything to avoid coming back after getting rejected by the trust company. The dogs were whining and a glance at the clock told me it was past feeding time. I poured them some dry food and fresh water and set about cleaning the house. It wasn't massive—with each room smaller than the next and just the two bedrooms upstairs. One and a half bathrooms. But for some reason it was never clean. A long time ago we employed a cleaning woman every other week. That kind of service disappeared when Adam took control of the finances.

Nira never understood why I enjoyed cleaning. I just let the lemony chemicals lure my mind away to some fantasy place while my body did the dirty work. Just like when the clock hit 5:00 and I'd pour myself a gin and tonic, allowing the alcohol to numb the emptiness and boredom I felt on a daily basis.

Once the house shined to an appropriate level of perfection, I sat on the couch facing the front door with Mo curled up on the throw pillow next to me. Maxie was napping in my bedroom. While I relaxed and waited on my spouse, I felt that the roles were reversed. Adam would answer to me this time.

*

Money was the number one argument between Adam and me—and we were out of baby food for Nira. She was screaming into my ear as I rocked her. She never screamed. I cradled her in my arms and hustled out of the house to the supermarket down the street. When we arrived at the store, I realized I didn't have any cash and wrote a check.

I got Nira home, settled her into the highchair, and served her some mashed carrots. I fell into a kitchen chair. At least I didn't have too much on the agenda for the rest of the day. Nira went back to her calm-baby self after having a few bites. Poor thing. For the most part, she was a fuss-less child. She smiled at me with more carrot on her face than in her mouth. Her cheeks looked like apples. The rest of the day was normal—just Nira and I moving around the house.

At 4:00 PM I put Nira down for a late nap and decided to get a head start on dinner. I was making spaghetti and meatballs—the meatballs from scratch. Special ingredient: love. Well, love-making. Adam was always extra feisty after his favorite meal.

I wasn't yet cooking in my dream kitchen, but I was cooking for my dream family. Adam's company was booming and we'd been living in

Weston for two years. We had plans to make our humble house into a warm, welcoming home—one that people wanted to be in, be comforted by. A house different than the one I grew up in.

I was molding the ground beef into perfect round balls when the front door slammed against the wall. It startled me enough that I dropped the beef and it made a splat as it hit the counter. I wiped my hands on my apron and headed down the hall to the front door.

Adam was seated in the formal living room. We never used that room. The furniture was soft, velvety. Expensive. I smiled at Adam. Although he'd put on a little weight since we graduated college, he still had muscle definition that could take my breath away—like a God's. He wore his dark brown hair pulled back into a ponytail but still appeared manly.

"I came home early," he said and leaned forward, his face blank.

"I can see that." The smiled dropped from my face. "What's wrong?"

"Did you write a check today?"

"What?" I laughed. I shouldn't have. I knew how angry it made him to be laughed at. I knew how serious he was about money. Our arguments about money were intense, fist clenching, knuckle whitening exchanges that somehow remained respectable, just a small notch above even-tempered.

Adam shook his head. He was behaving strangely—even in anger he cracked a joke or two.

I sat on the chaise across from him.

"Did you write a check today?" he repeated.

"Yes. I had to buy food for the baby." I didn't understand the question. Why shouldn't I write a check?

"Where is the baby?" He stood and paced. Small, deliberate steps.

"She's napping." I crossed my legs and watched Adam walk back and forth across the room. My heart twitched.

"Good." He cracked his knuckles, which I hated. I knew better than to tell him to cut it out. He stopped pacing and stood in front of me. "Aren't you supposed to ask me before you spend any money?"

"Well, I thought I could tell you when you got home from work."

"No, not tell me. *Ask* me."

And so it began. I wanted to say something about how our child was crying from hunger. About how we were a team and that his money was also mine and vice versa. He'd always been most liberal when it came to spending money on himself, but he also rarely questioned my own financial actions. Until today.

He sat back down and faced me. "Well?"

I could feel the hot, hidden rage bubbling from under his skin. Whatever I said would be wrong. "I'm sorry."

"Yeah," he said and laughed. It was a nasty laugh. "You don't respect me at all." His voice grew tight, even a little high. His blood pressure was probably through the roof.

"I do. I didn't... I guess I wasn't thinking." I was such an idiot. Why hadn't I called him before writing the check?

"Why do you have to be so fucking stupid?"

My right eye twitched at the same time my mouth fell open. While we'd argued about money before, it never resorted to name-calling. I tensed. I may not have thought things out but he didn't have to be so damn mean.

"You're not going to respond?" The veins pulsed from his forehead— I could almost hear them. I'd never seen him look so horrid. "Jesus, at least try to defend yourself."

I couldn't. He was acting crazy. What do you say to a crazy man?

"Your father was right. You're pathetic. Not worth a thing."

My father is a hateful man. I never expected my husband to act the same way. I looked at the floor, studied the plush carpet. I heard the creaking of the chair as he stood. Then I was looking at his feet. I refused to look up.

"You disgust me." He left the room. He must've been playing with Nira because I heard her giggle.

This was not how I expected things to be with Adam.

But I did nothing.

*

I wondered who I would be if I'd done things differently. I thought of Rick and how maybe he could've been the one to make me happy. The keys turned in the front door and Mo jumped off the couch to get a better look. I didn't need a peek, still didn't know what I was going to say. I'd been at a loss for words a lot lately.

The door opened and Adam stepped inside. Mo took a few sniffs and then settled at my feet. Adam halted as soon as he noticed me sitting stiff and upright on the sofa. We held each other's eyes long enough for me to feel my cheeks flush. I still loved him, but that wasn't enough anymore. It ceased being enough years ago.

"Why you just sitting there?" he barked at me.

"Waiting for you to get home."

"Really?" He scratched his head before plopping into his leather chair. He opened the day old newspaper that rested folded at his feet. "Did you miss me or something?"

What a loaded question. I missed who he used to be. I missed when he worked hard and was proud of himself and didn't sit in his chair all day taking out his hatred for himself on me and our children. But that was a long time ago. That was before he had the stroke and was declared unable to work, before we started living off his disability. I stood by him for everything, stood there until my feet were raw. But now the skin was back. I was back.

"We need to talk." Dreaded words no one liked to hear.

Adam rested the paper on his lap. "Is something wrong? Something happen to Sarah or Eric?" His forehead crinkled.

I believed his concern. I knew he was heartbroken over Nira, even though he didn't know how to show it. Properly expressing emotions was never one of his strong points.

"They're fine." I felt fine, too. I wasn't even angry anymore. "Where'd you go earlier?"

"For a ride."

"Did you visit the museum?" Adam often spent time wandering around the Hudson River Museum. It was his one hobby, the one thing that made him almost human.

"Yeah."

"Were there a lot of people?"

"No, not really."

I crossed my ankles. "When did you decide to forge my signature?"

"What?" Adam almost knocked the newspaper off his lap. It wasn't difficult to catch him off guard. Once he was a bright man, but that light long since dimmed.

"I know what you tried to do, Adam."

"I don't know what you're talking about." He spewed balls of spit when he talked, large globs I could make out from across the room. I didn't buy it. It'd been a long time since I'd bought his bullshit.

"The trust company called me."

"And?"

I don't know why he was playing dumb. It never got him anywhere before. "They called to tell me that you tried to gain access. Why'd you think you'd get away with it?"

"Oh. Shut. Up." He separated each word with a brief pause, as if in pain, and tugged at his ponytail.

"No, I will not. You can't just take things without asking."

Adam shifted from one butt cheek to the other. "I did ask."

"And I said I wasn't sure what I wanted to do with the money yet. I didn't say go ahead and forge my name and try to take the money for yourself."

"What's the big fucking deal?" His face turned red as it swelled with anger and blood. "I worked and you spent my money. You never worked; you just sat at home on your ass."

This old argument again. "That's not the point. The money isn't yours to take."

"Don't tell me what to do and shut the fuck up."

"Why? Why can't I ever speak?" I scratched at my arm.

"Because everything you have to say is so fucking stupid."

"No, it's not. I'm not stupid. You're an asshole." My arm was bleeding.

"Didn't I say shut the fuck up?"

I stood. "I'm not doing this anymore. I want you to leave."

"What the hell are you talking about?"

"This. Us. I'm done. And you need to go." I almost stomped my foot for emphasis.

"Yeah, okay." He laughed at me. "Sure," Adam said and hoisted himself from the chair. "I'm going to Bodhran Pub." His favorite bar was a few streets over. "But I'll be back. This is my home. If you don't want to be with me, then you leave." He walked out of the house with a cloud of immaturity billowing behind him.

I climbed the stairs to my bedroom, Mo at my feet. I felt light, airy. Even though I knew Adam didn't believe me. He would expect me to be home when he came back. His home, as he called it. If anyone's blood and sweat went into this house, it was mine. I took a large suitcase and a duffel bag from my closet because, this time, what I had in the trunk of my car wasn't going to be enough. Even if it broke my heart, I was leaving. I was going into the city to stay with Ruby, my best friend. Elsa may have lived in a mansion, but she had Billy to care for, to keep her company. Ruby had no one at home. She would welcome me with open arms and I would have no choice but to walk straight into them.

Maxie barked at me from the daybed. The dogs always knew what the suitcases meant. But this time they were wrong. I wasn't going to leave them with Adam, leave them behind. This time was for real and they were coming with me.

Chapter 5

I dialed the number to Rick's office. It was getting easier and easier to contact him. The secretary didn't scare me anymore; she didn't affect me at all. She said nothing when I requested Rick and connected me. "Janie." Rick's voice was so warm I felt cuddled by him. "How are you?"

"I need your help, again." I hadn't asked for help in so many years and now it seemed as if that was all I was doing. Cashing in on favors. Rick owed me for breaking my heart the summer before college. My parents didn't like him because he wasn't Jewish and wouldn't let me out of the house often enough to see him. He needed more attention than I could give.

"I don't remember you being this helpless when we were younger. In fact, I remember you bossing Elsa and Gabriella around as if you were their mother," he said and laughed. It sounded more old and tired than I remembered.

I laughed, too. "I was protecting them."

"From whom? I'm pretty sure Gabriella did more damage to the boys at Lincoln High than they did to her."

By that point I laughed so hard I snorted. The snort put an end to my laughter, but Rick continued with his for a little longer. I cleared my throat. "So."

"Sorry," he said, chuckling one last time. "How can I help you?"

After years of going back and forth, it had taken my daughter's death to push me into making the decision. "It's time for me to leave Adam."

Thick silence. Forget cutting it with a knife—you'd need a saw.

"Okay," Rick said, taking the reins. "Do you want me to represent you?"

"There's more. He forged the form to try to gain access to the trust account. I think I want to press charges."

"I think that would be a good idea."

"I was actually hoping you could suggest someone else. I don't think it'd be appropriate if you were my lawyer." Because Adam would throw a tantrum that would embarrass a two year old.

"Right. All right. Let me think of a list of the best lawyers and see who's available. I'll give you a call, okay?"

"Sure. You can either call my cell or reach me at Ruby's."

"You're at Ruby's?"

"Yes, let me give you the number."

Rick continued to talk while he jotted down the number. "I can't believe you still talk to Ruby."

I smiled. Funny, Ruby couldn't believe I was talking to Rick.

"Okay, I'll call you in a couple of days."

"Thanks for everything, Rick."

"Well, you owe me now." The beep that followed told me the conversation was over.

*

"When are you going home this time?" Sarah asked as she shoveled macaroni and cheese into her mouth. She and Eric came to New York City to visit me so I treated them to dinner at a posh place downtown. The food she inhaled was pricey enough to have been made from gold—loaded with cheeses I couldn't pronounce and andouille sausages. Not something she should be shoveling.

"You're disgusting," Eric said and tried not to look at Sarah. "Use a napkin for chrissake." He pulled a cloth napkin from the table and chucked it at his sister.

"Hey," I said in a low tone only mothers have mastered. "Let's try to act like adults, okay?"

Eric laughed. "There are no adults here."

Sarah kept on shoveling.

Eric and I stopped talking and continued to enjoy our own food. I was having filet mignon. It was the first piece of decent steak I'd had in over thirty years. Adam always insisted I buy the cheap meat and then complained when it tasted like cardboard.

The restaurant was of a higher caliber than I was used to—not one that Adam and I had gone to before. Mirrors lined the walls and bounced light around the small, dim room. The rest of the clientele wore freshly pressed suits and designer labels I couldn't pronounce. I fingered the fraying wool neckline of my oversized sweater and vowed to go shopping soon.

Sarah choked on some pasta and dropped her fork. She shook the table as she reached for a glass of water.

Eric and I put our utensils down and watched. This was nothing new, Sarah eating too fast and choking. It was a habit of her father's as well, naturally. Eric patted her on the back and rolled his eyes at me. I shrugged.

"I'm good, I'm good," Sarah said and wiped the tears from her eyes.

I didn't wait any longer for her to gather herself. I didn't want my melt-in-your-mouth steak to get cold and hard.

Before Eric resumed eating, he repeated Sarah's question: "When are you going home this time?"

"I'm not." And this was why I'd really invited them out for dinner to a fancy restaurant—both because I felt guilty and because I was hoping they would choose not to make a scene in public.

Sarah raised an eyebrow and dropped her jaw. "You're not what?"

Eric elbowed her. "She's not going back to Dad. Are you really going to press charges against him for forgery?"

29

I scratched through the thick wool to my raw elbow. "No, I'm not going home. Maxie and Mo are with me at Ruby's." I took a sip of my gin and tonic.

"You're kidding." Sarah was no longer smiling. "Why?"

"You know why, Sarah."

"No," she said and shook her head. "We all agreed you would never leave."

I choked back a bitter laugh. I didn't care what they all "agreed" or what anyone thought of me. It was my turn to be selfish. Finally.

"So what, is this like a trial separation or what?" Eric asked. He continued to eat.

"No. I'm done. This is it." I wiped my mouth with the cloth napkin. "And I think I am going to press charges, yes."

"This is all because Nira left you money," Sarah said. "That fucking bitch."

"Don't," I said and pushed my plate away. I was full. The last bite of steak rested, a weight on my tongue. It was gristle and impossible to chew.

"She's not here anymore, Mom. She can't tell you what to do." Sarah crossed her arms over her chest.

Part of the reason that Sarah and Nira didn't get along was because of me. Nira was bossy. She liked to be in control. When Nira was around, sometimes I had the energy to stand up for myself. Adam and Sarah always held it against Nira when I spoke up. Well, they couldn't hold it against her anymore. It wouldn't be fair—the dead can't stick up for themselves.

"It's not because of Nira," I said. "Yes, her money helps. But she isn't exactly here to tell me what to do, is she?"

Sarah moved her plate away. "Dad can't survive without you. He can't take care of himself. Are you trying to teach him a lesson or something?"

"That's not my fault, Sarah. Daddy... he's not an old man. He'll have to figure it out. I'm not a maid." I scratched my arm. "I'm not trying to teach him a lesson. I just want to be happy."

"But she's right, Mom," Eric said. "And what if he does time? Is that what you want?"

It killed me to think about sending the father of my children to prison. That wasn't my intention. I still loved him very much. Even missed him. But if I didn't do something he would continue walking around breaking the law.

"I have to," I said.

Sarah forced her chair from the table with a bang. "Eric, can I have the car keys? I'll wait for you."

Eric reached into his pants pocket and tossed the keys to Sarah.

"No," I said, the pleading tickling at my throat. "Sarah, don't go."

But my only living daughter walked away. I thought that she would understand. Nira would've been on my side because she wanted me to be happy, even though she had more memories of the good days than Sarah. The good days were the most painful to remember.

*

Nira was the perfect little girl. Just a few weeks after she was born, Adam and I were able to take her out to four-star restaurants—something we stopped doing after the twins came along. Sometimes she would sleep and sometimes she would just watch us. She was always well behaved. Since Nira was born in the '80s, she was subject to some traumatizing hairstyles. Or so she used to remind me constantly. She had a short, boy's haircut, which I thought looked adorable, for most of her youth. I was keeping her in style.

Adam and Nira had monthly dates. It was moments like those that made Adam a good father, made me remember why I married him.

Nira just started picking out her own clothes. She was seven years old and hated pants. Her closet was full of what she referred to as party dresses. Dressing her up was like playing with the dolls I never had a chance to actually play with—they were reserved for Gabriella.

"Can I wear this one, Mommy?" She pulled a blue and pink floral dress with a satin collar from the closet.

"Of course," I said.

I could hear Adam in the shower down the hall, humming loudly. He loved his dates with Nira. It would be a shame when she outgrew them.

Nira sat in front of her closet and started tossing around shoes. The obsessive neatness to her personality wouldn't develop for several more years.

"Woah there," I said and sat next to her. "What pair are you looking for?"

"Shiny white with a bow," she said. "I can't find them anywhere!"

Better act fast. Nira could be explosive at times. Especially when things were out of her control.

"It's okay, we'll find them." I moved her snow boots aside and discovered the white shoes. They were not as shiny as I expected. In fact, they were covered in black scuffs. I was reluctant to show them to her.

"Yay!" she yelled and grabbed them from me. "Ew. They look terrible!" Nira opened her small eyes wide and tears collected at the corners.

"Hold on," I said and left her whimpering on the carpet. I went into the bathroom and pulled cotton swabs and nail polish remover from the medicine cabinet. My mother had taught me a few successful tips. With a little pressure I used the cotton swab soaked in nail polish remover to erase the marks on Nira's pretty white shoes. Once they looked good as new I brought them back to Nira's room.

She jumped up from her spot in front of the closet, ran over to me, and grabbed the shoes. "I guess this will be okay," she said and offered a weak smile.

I sat on her bed and watched as her little hands pulled up the opaque white tights. She struggled but didn't ask for help. I rose and tugged the tights the rest of the way up, assisted her with stepping into the dress, and buttoned up the back. She wanted to put the shoes on all by herself. It only took her one extra try.

She looked like a little grown-up.

Adam appeared at the door in a black pinstriped suit and shiny black loafers. He was clean-shaven, youthful. His smile warmed me to the core.

"Daddy, do I look pretty?" Nira twirled and her dress flew around her.

Adam laughed. "You look beautiful."

"And you look handsome," Nira said.

He took her hand and looked at me. "Well, we're off."

"Have a good time," I said.

I watched them walk hand in hand from the room.

*

The good couldn't outweigh the bad anymore. I looked my grown son right in the eye and said, "This is about me. She's just being Sarah, and that's her choice, but you two are adults now and it's time for me to focus on myself."

I waived the waiter over and asked for the check.

Eric nodded and took a large gulp of iced water. "This is going to cause a lot of drama."

"Well, I'm sorry for that." And I was. I didn't want Eric and Sarah to suffer because of my choice to leave their father. But they would have to accept it, move on. Maybe someday even support me in my decisions. I never claimed to be perfect. I was only human.

The waiter brought the check and placed it before me. I took out my wallet and paid in cash. It was a new feeling, paying with my own money, even if it was passed on to me by my deceased daughter. Nira was still there for me.

Eric and I stood and walked from the restaurant. Sarah was seated in the passenger's seat of Eric's car and wouldn't look at me. I took a step toward the car and Eric put his arm out to stop me, shaking his head.

"Give her some time, Mom. I wouldn't talk to her right now. Like you said, she's just being Sarah. She's only going to say something hurtful."

He was right. I'd let Sarah cool off, give her time to remember how miserable life was for me with her father. Let her learn not to be selfish for once. I let Eric go without forcing a hug on him, figuring the announcement of his parent's divorce coupled with physical interaction would be too much. I watched my children drive away and climbed into my own car.

I'd left my cell phone on the passenger seat when I'd gone into the restaurant and now it blinked to let me know there was a new voicemail. I played the message. Rick had called with a referral. And to ask me out to dinner. I wasn't surprised. I knew there would always be chemistry between us, but that didn't mean dating Rick was a good idea. Before I could talk myself out of it further I dialed his number to call back with a "Thank you" and a "Yes".

Chapter 6

Rick offered to go to the lawyer's office with me. I declined. I was addicted to my newfound independence. I felt high from it and my blood ran quicker with the satisfaction of doing things on my own.

I never enjoyed the company of lawyers. While growing up there were always a lot of lawyers and doctors around the house, my parents' friends. They were rich, snobby creatures and because of their presence, our parents demanded perfect behavior from my sisters and me. I cringed when Rick chose the law as his profession—suspicious he would turn into one of them.

David Wrentham, the lawyer that had me seated in his waiting room, was an old friend of Rick's—someone who would be doing Rick a personal favor by representing me in my divorce and pressing criminal charges against Adam for forging access to the trust.

A short, round man entered the waiting room. Under the fluorescent light, beads of sweat glistened like jewels on his forehead. "Mrs. Brown?"

I nodded and stood. "Nice to meet you Mr. Wrentham." We shook hands and I recoiled when his slimy palm slid against my dry one.

"Likewise," he said and held out his arm, gesturing toward his office.

The office was tacky. The walls were made of cheap wood paneling—it looked like my grandparents' basement when I was a child. I noticed similar panels lined the floor before I realized that all of the furniture was the same faded, fake wood.

We each sat in a worn brown leather chair.

A woman as round as Mr. Wrentham entered the room with a platter of drinks. "Would you like some water or coffee?" she asked.

"This is my wife," Mr. Wrentham explained.

I nodded at her and helped myself to a glass of water. "Thank you," I said.

"Call if you need anything." Mrs. Wrentham gave a dimpled smile and toddled off down the hall.

Mr. Wrentham pushed a coaster across the table and I put my glass down.

"So Rick tells me you want to file divorce papers and press criminal charges against your husband?"

I nodded.

"All right," he said and picked up a legal pad from the desk. "I'm going to ask a lot of questions, some that may make you uncomfortable. Just try to answer them as best you can and let me know if you need to take a break."

"Sure." I could handle that, right?

"How long have you been married?"

"Thirty-two years." Too long. "But we've been together for forty-one." Even hindsight hadn't helped—during nine years of courtship I'd missed all the signs that Adam would turn into such a beast of a man.

"And three children?"

"Yes. Well, I have two now. One passed away recently." I twitched a little. Maybe it actually would've been a good idea to bring someone with me, someone to hold my hand. I was stronger than I thought possible, but didn't even I deserve someone to lean on?

"My apologies." Mr. Wrentham and I made eye contact. He opened his mouth as if to say something more but stopped, instead flapping his lips together like a fish breathing in air rather than water. "Is she the one you inherited money from? Rick didn't provide me with all of the details."

I nodded. "Yes."

Mr. Wrentham shifted in his chair. I wondered who was more uncomfortable. He proceeded to ask me questions about pressing charges against Adam in the past and I explained that he'd never been charged with anything as an adult before. I told him that the forgery was criminal behavior I needed to take action against.

"Has he committed other similar acts?" Mr. Wrentham asked.

This was awkward. I was having trouble breathing. "He has signed my name to other things. Credit card applications, mortgage statements..."

"And no criminal record?"

"He told me he went to juvenile detention for assault years ago. He was an unpopular child, a victim of foster care really, and went after one of his bullies with a knife."

"But this is the first time you've felt the need to press charges?"

Was that so difficult to believe? "Our relationship has been... sour for years. But I never thought of him as a criminal. He's my husband. He's always had somewhat questionable behavior, but I never expected things to get this bad."

"Can you give some examples of this questionable behavior?"

I laughed, but the sound that came out was deep, angry. Unlike any noise I'd made before. "He's done the same thing to our children—opened accounts under their names and ruined their credit."

"Okay. Would you say the relationship has always been tumultuous?"

"Not always, but for a long time now."

"Has there ever been any physical abuse?"

I knew he would ask that. I took too long to answer, making my reply known before the word left my mouth. "Once."

"What happened?"

"He pushed me off the bed." Although I was here to separate myself from Adam, I still didn't want to make him out to be the devil. I didn't want to tell Mr. Wrentham my husband pushed me in front of our child, made her witness to his atrocious behavior.

"Do you have any evidence or witnesses?"

If I told him Sarah was there would he make her be a witness? I didn't want that. But if I didn't reveal every detail maybe the whole thing would fall apart. Maybe I'd have to stay. I couldn't do that, could I? I closed my eyes and took a deep breath. "My youngest daughter was there. I don't think that Adam would've laid a hand on her, but we left for the night just in case." I opened my eyes and stared hard at Mr. Wrentham. "And I don't want her involved in this."

"Well, we'll do our best not to have her involved. How old was she at the time of the altercation?"

"She was twelve then."

"In all likelihood we will not need to involve her in any of this. Can you tell me if you ever physically fought back?"

The blood pumped through my veins. Not many people knew that the calm, cool, and collected woman they see now is not the woman that existed years ago. That woman did not regularly take anti-depressants and anti-anxiety medication, did not force her husband to pay for them despite his verbal abuse.

"Most of the time I walked away or went to my sister's house just to avoid him. But I did get frustrated with him sometimes. One time when he was being difficult, when I was being instigated more than I could handle, I tried to punch him. I missed and broke my thumb."

"Did he press charges against you for attempted assault?"

"What? No. He laughed. I drove myself to the hospital."

"Did it happen often—you taking your frustrations out physically?"

"No, not often. I threw things sometimes."

"All right. How are things financially? Why would he feel the need to take money from you?"

"Adam's all about money. When he started to lose his company he fell apart."

"How did he lose the company?"

"He never told me point blank. But from overhearing conversations I'd have to say it's because he was investing money with the wrong kind of people. Then one day he sold 51% of the company. It seemed to me one day we were fine and then we suddenly had nothing."

"By fine do you mean financially stable?"

Things had rarely been stable. "I guess we were comfortable. It's hard to explain. Adam always had money for himself. Still does. It was the rest of us that suffered."

Mr. Wrentham nodded his head. "May I ask why you stayed?"

"The usual reasons. I love him, and he's the father of my children."

He put his notebook down on the desk and scooted forward in his seat. "I know how difficult this is, Mrs. Brown. I want you to know I will be by your side through these proceedings."

I stared at him, unsure of what to say. This was more personal than I expected, more like a therapy session than I was ready for. I opened my mouth but nothing came out. I closed it—I must have looked like a very stupid woman to Mr. Wrentham.

He picked up the notebook and leaned back in his seat. "So, we have criminal charges for forgery and attempted theft. Then we have divorce charges based on irreconcilable differences. Do you know if your husband has a divorce attorney yet?"

"I don't think my husband believes I'll go through with a divorce," I said and scratched the back of my hand.

"Why do you say that?"

"Because I never had the guts to do it before."

"And you do now?"

"Yes." My daughter gave me strength.

"And you're sure you want to go through with this? With everything?"

"Yes." I didn't hesitate.

Mr. Wrentham placed the pad on his desk. "I can't promise that this will be easy. In fact, it may be painful and grueling at times. But you'll get through this and be stronger for it. My office will arrange to have Mr. Brown served. Will your husband contest the divorce?"

"Probably."

"Then we will need to request a preliminary conference, but can discuss that more later. I think it's best that we take things one step at a time. That will mean a separate case for the forgery."

"I understand," I said.

"The proceedings may take a long time. Are you prepared for how draining it could be?"

How could I be? All I could do was my best. That's all I could ever do. I nodded.

"All right then. I'll get the paperwork together for the divorce and be in touch about the forgery charges."

I felt like I'd lost at least five pounds. Although I suppose I lost closer to two hundred and fifteen—Adam's full weight.

"Thank you so much." I leaned forward to shake Mr. Wrentham's hand but he stood and walked around the desk.

He extended his arms out and I stood, letting him embrace me with his large, moist body. He was a kind man. I wasn't used to it.

Chapter 7

I reluctantly climbed into my car for a field trip to my parents' house. It was time to tell them that I was leaving Adam. So far, I'd managed to keep them oblivious to it all—they didn't even know I was staying with Ruby. It hadn't been easy because they were located just five minutes from my house. But since my father had Alzheimer's my parents didn't go out much.

I pulled up in front of their house and parked. Over the years the front lawn had started to brown and eventually my parents hired a gardener. My mother was never one to dwell outdoors so she escaped that duty. The gardener did a nice job, somehow managing to have colorful flowers blooming around a home that was so dead and dark on the inside. My father even had a bird feeder planted in the back. How he could love animals more than his own family I'd never know.

They didn't know anything yet, but I could already sense their disapproval. I wasn't their first daughter to get divorced and they'd never been Adam's biggest fans, but I knew they weren't going to react favorably. I tried to inhale deep, calm breaths, but the focus on my breathing just made me more nervous.

"Screw this." I stepped out of the car. I was far too old to be so terrified of my parents.

The steps to their front door were slippery from the recent rain. I was grateful that my father succumbed to installing the sturdy iron ramp and using the wheelchair when going out. A purple and green mezuzah sparkled outside the door. I mumbled, "Hear, O Israel, the Lord our God, the Lord is One" and let myself into the house. It was dark and smelled moldy. My mother never opened the windows because of the killer germs located outside.

"Hello?" I couldn't be sure which room they were in and I didn't want to stumble upon my father in his underwear. It had happened before and it wasn't pretty.

"Who's there?" My mother already sounded like she was in a bad mood. Fantastic.

"Janie."

"Oh, hi." Her voice warmed a bit and with it my heart stopped pounding so hard. She came around the corner. Her frail arms wrapped as far around me as they could reach.

I followed her into the living room. "Where's Dad?"

"Sleeping."

He was always sleeping. I didn't envy her. Sixty-five years of a miserable marriage and now she was condemned to being a nursemaid. My father always wanted everything perfect, everything done his way. Mother kept her mouth closed and obeyed.

"How are you? What's new?" she asked. We sank into the overstuffed sofa.

I wasn't hungry, but dipped my hand into the candy bowl that overflowed on the coffee table. My father had been a health nut most of my life. Now he lived off sweets.

"Not much." Oh good, start off with a lie. "How's Dad doing?"

She flinched as if she'd been jabbed or poked. "He's the same. Doesn't really know what's going on. He peed in the closet again last night."

"What does the doctor say?" I asked.

"That I shouldn't be doing everything on my own and need a nurse."

"Like Elsa and I have told you. And? Are you going to get some help?"

Her already thin lips disappeared when she pressed them together. "You know Father won't allow it."

"Of course not."

"Don't start."

"I'm not." It took me years to realize that I needed to leave my husband. I had long been telling my mother to do the same—far before my father fell ill. But she was old-fashioned and would have nothing to do with divorce.

"How are Sarah and Eric?"

"They're fine," I answered. "Eric just got another promotion at work."

"That's great. I wish he would've called to tell me himself."

"He has a lot going on, Mom."

"Mmmhmm."

Oh God, how Nira and I hated that sound. How we laughed and mimicked it. My mother made noises to demonstrate emotion. This one was judgment. Time to get this over with.

"I actually came over to tell you that I've left Adam."

"What?"

Another one of my pet peeves with Mother. She refused to wear her hearing aide. You could never really tell if she couldn't hear you or was just pretending. "I left Adam. I'm staying with Ruby"

"I don't understand. Why would you leave? Why aren't you staying at your sister's?" Her voice grew nasally and high. It made nails on a chalkboard sound like beautiful music.

I tensed, my arms rigid by my side. "You know why I left." Everyone in the family knew how Adam was, they just chose to ignore it. Just because my mother stayed with her husband didn't mean I had to do the same. "I'm at Ruby's because I didn't want to burden Elsa."

"He's your husband, Janie. You took a vow to always be at his side."

"I know what vow I took, Mom. But when I took that vow I didn't know that he was going to tear me down and belittle me my whole life."

"It doesn't matter. That vow is sacred."

My parents were hypocritically religious. They only went to temple on the high holidays but still managed to toss around how important religion was in the meantime.

"Okay, well, sacred or not I'm not going back. In fact," I took a deep breath, inhaled from the depth of my stomach and said, "I'm divorcing him."

"Janie. Don't be silly. Take some time apart if you need to but you can't destroy the relationship you've made together."

"It was destroyed a long time ago, Mom."

"Mmmhmm." She crossed her legs. "A woman should never leave her husband's side, just as I have always stuck by your father."

"We're different people. I've stayed long enough. I deserve to be happy."

"And what about your children?"

"My children are grown. They'll learn to live with it."

"And Nira? Would she have accepted this?"

Mother had no idea that Nira would've been jumping up and down with joy. And what was she getting at? Did I have my dead daughter's approval?

"Yes, she would have, but that doesn't really matter now." I hated arguing with mother, it was always easier to just agree. Easiest to shut up and agree with everyone.

"Of course it matters, because you shouldn't be doing this."

"Mom. Please. Can you just be supportive this one time?"

"What is that supposed to mean?"

"I just...I'm not changing my mind on this. I just want you to understand that."

"I don't want to hear any more about this, this ridiculous decision." She stood. "Do you want me to see if your father is awake?"

Why? So I could try to explain to him what was going on just so he would forget in five minutes? So he could tell me the mistake I made in marrying Adam in the first place? When Rick and I broke up my father told me, "Strike one." I could guess what he would say now without having to hear it.

"No, thanks."

My mother stood. "You'll see your father." She walked from the room.

I sat on the couch and waited. I could easily have escaped, but I didn't. Like the frightened twelve year-old child I used to be, I shrank into the couch and feared a confrontation with my father.

*

Gabriella, aged seven, ran outside the minute the yelling began. The first glass shattered against the wall and shards fell in a rainbow, catching the light while sprinkling all around us. Elsa and I stayed believing the argument wouldn't escalate. We were wrong.

My father accused my mother of having another boyfriend. Such accusations were not unusual and went both ways. When mother denied it, father threw glass after glass into the kitchen wall. Bits and pieces bounced off Elsa and me.

I grabbed Elsa's hand and pulled her into the hallway, toward the front door.

"No," she squealed and wiggled away. "I don't want to go outside!"

"El," I said and gave her my most grown-up look. "Let's go outside and play with Gabriella." I could hear my mother sobbing. She cried deep, breathy sobs from the pit of her stomach.

Elsa looked back toward the kitchen. "Can we check on Mommy?" she asked me.

Heavy footsteps stomped around the other room. "Stop your crying," my father demanded. The footsteps stopped, and then changed direction.

"We can check on her later." I snatched Elsa's hand a second time and yanked her from the house before she could put up a fight.

Once outside, Elsa tore herself from me and ran to Gabriella, who was standing on the other side of the fence.

I ran toward them.

"Are they still yelling?" Gabriella asked.

"It snowed glass," Elsa told her.

Gabriella bit her lip in confusion and looked at me.

"Dad threw a juice glass."

Blood welled from the corner of her mouth.

"Ew," Elsa said and pointed at our sister.

I reached into my pocket and pulled out a handkerchief. "Jeez, Gab," I wiped the blood from Gabriella's lip and glanced back at the house. "What'd you go and do that for?"

"I didn't mean to!" she snapped. "Are we just going to stand here?"

"Girls!" My father yelled from the front steps.

Gabriella took off down the street. Elsa and I stayed glued to the sidewalk.

"Get inside this instant!"

Elsa tugged at my arm. I couldn't bear to look at her, to see her innocent little face. I didn't know what to do. Whether we followed

41

Gabriella or stayed we would be in trouble for leaving the house without permission. Once again I pulled Elsa along, although this time she was weak, helpless. A ragdoll. She knew what was coming.

Hand in hand we walked up the stone stairs to our house. Our father stayed in the doorway until we climbed the steps and even then he only shifted slightly, just enough so we could squeeze by and into the house.

He banged the door behind us and slipped the belt from his pants, snapping it against his open palm.

I shivered.

*

When my father entered the room I didn't recognize him. It had been like that since Gabriella died. He was a shriveled up little man, yet he still terrified me. Each step was pained, his feet almost incapable of lifting off the ground. He collapsed into a reclining chair.

"Gabriella?" He squinted his eyes and looked away.

She'd been his favorite.

"No," my mother said, an unfamiliar gentleness to her tone. "It's Janie, see?" She softly pressed two fingers under his chin and guided his face toward me.

My father looked at me with glassy eyes. "Yes, Janie," he said, but his words were empty.

I had difficulty feeling bad for him after everything he'd put me through over the years. Elsa said I was cold. "How are you, Dad?"

He stared at my mother and back at me. "Get your sisters ready for school, Janie. I'm in no mood to wait."

My mother and I made eye contact. We both wore looks of disapproval. She didn't understand how I could leave my husband and I couldn't understand how she stayed.

Chapter 8

After a few weeks as Ruby's guest I couldn't take it anymore. I was bored and she wouldn't let me clean. Since I couldn't live with Ruby forever I needed to find a job or maybe take some classes. Both of these ideas terrified me. It had been years—no, decades—since I'd been employed or gone to school. Instead, I labored over raising my three children and trying to maintain a nice home for them and my husband.

My husband. For just a little bit longer. Adam was served earlier in the week for divorce. As was to be expected, he didn't sign the papers and had no plans to. He would draw this out, long and tortured and bloody. I tried not to think about what would be the damage from the legal costs. I knew Mr. Wrentham was giving me a deal because I was a friend of Rick's, but if Adam dragged this on would all of my money disappear?

Eric reported that Adam was beside himself and, if even possible, drinking more than usual. Sarah was avoiding me, blaming me for the downfall of the family even though she should've seen this coming years ago.

Ruby was a sweetheart. She was a comfort, like a sister. But on top of being bored out of my mind I was afraid of overstaying my welcome. I thought maybe if I showed some effort at fixing my life that she'd let me stick around for a bit longer.

For a long time I hated driving, hated even being in cars. Adam drove like a lunatic and I did everything to avoid being in the same car as him. But now, so close to being single and independent, I loved my alone time in the car. I liked to roll the window down and feel the wind comb through my hair, to bump along the road listening to oldies music that reminded me of better days. I looked forward to enjoying such a ride when I locked Ruby's door and walked downstairs to my car. Ruby was trying to rent me a spot in her building but for now I was parking on the street.

When I came in sight of my car, there was Adam, leaning against the front passenger's door, arms crossed, looking pathetic. He'd aged. His hair had more gray and his normally fat face was thin and ragged. I felt bad. It hurt me to hurt the man that I had once loved from the very core of my being. If I'd had the power to change things—but I didn't. And this is where we ended up.

"What are you doing here?" I asked. I walked away from Ruby's apartment building and closer to the car, wondering who told Adam that I was staying at Ruby's in the first place.

"This is all a joke, right?" he said and smiled. He smiled. I couldn't believe it. I knew he hadn't taken me seriously before I went to a lawyer, but now that he had the papers I thought he would realize this was really happening.

"C'mon, Adam. Just go home, okay? There's no reason for you to be here. If you have any questions you can talk to my lawyer." I wanted to get in the car and drive away, but with his bulbous frame blocking it that was impossible.

"Come home with me," he said, his tone softer, his face gentler. If I didn't know better I'd fall into his manipulative trap and be right back where I started.

"I'm never coming home," I said. Best to be blunt and not lead him on. I didn't want him thinking there was any hope left for us.

"Why not?" He crossed his arms.

I shook my head. There was no way that he could be this clueless—is what I would think if I didn't know him so well. I sighed, a part of me dying from sadness, a part of me so bitter and angry that I had no patience left. "I'm sorry," is all I said.

"I don't understand."

"No, you don't. How many times do we have to have the same conversation? I just can't do it anymore. I'm tired."

"So you end it, just like that?" He pulled himself away from the car and took a step toward me. "And you try to have me sent to fucking jail?" Despite the F-bomb his voice was still calmer than usual.

"Can we not do this? Can we just be adults?" I didn't want to, but I was pleading with him. Pleading a losing battle with an unreasonable, stubborn man.

Adam kicked around some dirt. "I love you, Janie."

"I love you, too, but it's just not enough. We're both miserable. Don't you want to be happy?"

"Cut the shit, Janie. Let's just forget about this. I forgive you for all the drama. Come home."

I fought the urge to laugh. "I didn't do this to hurt you," I said.

He looked angry then, more like himself. "You don't give a fuck. You're a cold, heartless bitch."

"Then why do you even want to be with me?" I asked. It didn't make any sense. If I made him as miserable as he made me, why the hell would he want to stay together?

"Stop acting stupid. We're married, we have children, we've built a life together."

"I know all this. And it's still not enough. Nothing you say can change my mind."

Adam looked like he was contemplating this, trying to figure out if it was true or not. His face distorted and he wore Nira's favorite look, the shit-eating face. He said, "If you want to play things this way I'll make your life a living hell."

"It already is," I answered without thinking. It was obvious there were a lot of reasons to leave this man. While kicking the rocks he walked far enough from the car that I was able to squeeze by and open the door. I looked back at him before climbing in. His mouth was slightly open, as if in shock, and he was still as stone. I felt tears pushing at the corner of my eyes, but I held them back. He didn't deserve them. I buckled myself in, pulled out of the space, and headed down the street. I wanted to turn around, to go back inside Ruby's apartment and crawl into a ball in the corner.

From the rearview mirror I watched Adam get into his car. And follow me. I tried to focus on the road but my eyes kept getting pulled back to the mirror and the maniac behind me. Why wouldn't he leave me alone? I slowed to a stop as I pulled up to a red light. Adam was still on my tail, approaching too fast for my liking. My hands were so sweaty they slid off the steering wheel. He stopped right before bumping my car. When the light turned green I did my best to speed off, which wasn't easy on any street in New York City. I forgot to breathe for a few seconds. He was still behind me. I didn't know if I should pull over or maybe head to the police station.

At the next light I skipped using my turn signal and took what I hoped was a sudden left. When I again looked in the rearview mirror he was still there. Bastard. I kept my eyes on the road while fumbling for my cell phone in the purse on the passenger seat. Maybe I could call someone for help. But who?

I reached another light and Adam pulled up beside me. He put his window down, so I did the same.

"What the hell, Adam?"

He stared at me, his face blank. Then he gave me the middle finger.

I had nothing to say to that and put my window back up. I looked straight ahead. When the light changed green he sped off and away, lost in the traffic.

I drove for a few more minutes then pulled over. What did he think he'd accomplish from doing something like that? I didn't understand why it was so hard for him to leave me alone. His days of terrorizing me should be over. He still thought he owned the world. He still thought he owned me.

*

I was balancing Maxie, who was just a puppy, on my hip and trying to pour food into Mo's bowl. The kids were all at school—Nira at the high school and Eric and Sarah down the street at the elementary school. Maxie always wanted to be held. We'd saved the dogs from an abusive home where they'd been kicked around. Mo was affectionate and outgoing but

Maxie often whimpered at her surroundings. Unable to grow a third arm I placed Maxie on the floor, close to Mo so she wouldn't feel so alone.

The phone rang and I grabbed it from the cradle on the wall. "Hello?"

"Janie." It was Adam. He sounded angry. "I'll be home early, soon." Adam's company was thriving and he often worked long hours. "I want cold beer in the fridge. We need to talk." He slammed the phone down.

I couldn't begin to fathom what Adam was angry about, but I knew enough for my palms to drench with sweat, for my breathing to grow shallow. There was no beer so I hurried out of the house and to the liquor store.

Adam still wasn't home when I returned so I put the six pack in the refrigerator and sat at the kitchen table. Sweating. Things were going so well. It was weeks since we'd argued, since the insults, the name-calling. For the life of me, I couldn't figure out what I could've done wrong.

The front door banged against the wall and then again into its frame. Maxie ran across the room and upstairs. She'd be hiding for hours.

Adam stomped into the room and went to the fridge. When he saw me seated at the kitchen table he grunted.

I was afraid to speak so instead I just stared. Sarah and Eric were sharing clothes and Adam stood before me in a five-hundred dollar suit.

"Aren't you going to ask me why I'm home early? How I am? What happened?" he said.

"What happened?" That's all I wanted to know.

Adam put the can down with a loud thud. "The company's screwed."

"What?" His company?

"I've had to sell 51%."

"What do you mean? I didn't know we were in trouble."

"We?" He laughed. "My company, Janie. That's why you didn't know—I didn't want you to. Anyway," he said, picking the beer back up and gulping it down, "as of today I only own 49%."

"But why?"

"I doubt you'd understand. Some stuff didn't pan out and then people wanted money back that I didn't have."

"So, you sold part of it?" I sounded dumb. Adam hated dumb questions, but I couldn't wrap my head around what was happening. At the beginning of our relationship Adam was a giver. He shared. It wasn't until after Nira was born that he took control of the finances. She needed attention and other things. And the other things cost money. Then I wasn't allowed to make the decisions about buying things for the home anymore and was cut out, forced to beg for every cent. So how was I to foresee Adam landing us in a place where he had to sell part of his business?

"Jesus, Janie. Shut the fuck up and listen to me. The company doesn't belong to me anymore. Got it?" He sat on a stool at the kitchen counter and glared at me.

Somehow this was my fault, although I wasn't sure how. I ground my teeth.

"You're not going to say anything?"

"What do you want me to say, Adam?"

"Aren't you sorry?"

"Yes, of course I'm sorry." Boy, was I sorry.

Adam opened the fridge and pulled out another beer, popped it open, and guzzled away. "This means things are going to change around here. We can't just spend money freely anymore."

Spend money freely? I'd never been able to do that. Never in my whole goddamn life. Adam was the one who always bought what he wanted. He was the one who draped himself in the finest clothes, who kept up on the most current technology. It was me and the kids that suffered in ratty clothing and old haircuts. Adam was always overdrawing the family bank account, but never had a problem finding money for those beautiful, shiny suits. There was talk for years, by my parents, about the possibility that Adam had a private bank account. I didn't think he was smart enough for that.

I don't know if he could read my face or he just lost it, but suddenly he was letting out a stream of curses that'd make a trucker wish he were deaf. "This is your fault. Your lack of support that made this happen."

"I'm sorry," I said.

"You're revolting. I hate you."

I couldn't help myself. "Well, you know what? I hate you, too." Just because I knew it was best to keep my mouth shut didn't mean I could always do so. I'd run out of my meds, or crazy pills as Adam called them, two weeks earlier and wasn't allowed to buy my refill. Again.

"Excuse me? Are you fucking kidding me? We wouldn't be in this mess if you'd ever had a job."

I laughed. It tasted bitter. I never worked because we'd agreed that I wouldn't. The familiar words rolled off my tongue. "I've been raising the children, Adam." My voice was even, untouched. I sounded calmer than I felt. Never a good sign.

"You've been lazy, spending my money, sleeping around."

I exhaled and said, for the millionth time, "We agreed I would stay at home."

He shook his head and beads of sweat flew around the room. "You should've worked."

It was like talking to a wall. Did he even hear me? Did he even try? I didn't want to waste my breath on this argument again. What was the point? I headed out of the kitchen.

"Hey, Fatty," Adam called after me.

I kept walking and he kept yelling after me. He followed me into the living room and stood against the staircase so I couldn't move past him.

"What do you want from me?" I asked. He probably wanted blood.

"Take some fucking responsibility, for chrissake. I didn't make this mess myself."

"Yes, you did." I don't know why I was speaking back to him. It would just prolong the argument. But I'd already tried to walk away and now I was trapped. Trapped in so many ways.

"You're a lazy, fat bitch, Janie. You always will be. Just look at you!"

I didn't think, I just swung. I never hit another human being in my life and I don't know what possessed me to do it this time. But I did. And I missed. Well, I missed Adam. My clenched fist collided with the oak stair banister, shattering my thumb.

I didn't even feel the physical pain. I just wanted to run away.

*

I tapped my hand on the steering wheel in beat to the music. I was revved up from my car chase with Adam and needed to calm down, maybe bury myself in a good book. I pulled into a parking garage down the street from the New York Public Library. I really needed to start taking public transportation—these parking rates were going to eat through Nira's trust. Maybe if I hid underground Adam wouldn't be able to find me.

It was a short walk to the library filled with interesting people and a fat squirrel I almost tripped over. The library was massive and my favorite of all the libraries I've been to. It was made of stone and had a domineering lion guarding the entrance. I found the lion comforting.

Once inside the library I made my way to the Fiction section. I was looking for anything by Stephen King because I wanted to immerse myself in a story more horrific than my own. I chose an older novel, one he wrote as Richard Bachman, about a boy involved in school shootings. Not the most uplifting but at least it was a page-turner—at least it was distracting. Stephen King had always been my favorite author, had always been successful in whisking me away from the real world. I settled into an oversized chair by a large window. If I hadn't been interrupted by a warm, familiar voice I would've stayed lost in King's world for hours.

"Janie?"

I peeked over the cover of my book.

"It is you!" A woman said, too loudly for a library. She was shorter than me with tight chocolate curls framing her face—a face I instantly recognized.

"Leah?" I tossed the book on the table next to me and jumped out of my chair. I had to bend slightly to give her a hug.

"How have you been?" she exclaimed.

Someone perusing the books down one of the aisles gave us a dirty look and said, "Shh."

I motioned for Leah to sit down and was seated next to her. Leah also went to SUNY and sang in the choir with me. She had a deep, throaty voice that captivated the audience. For a while we were close, but Adam didn't like her so we grew apart. Leah never took any of Adam's shit.

"You look fantastic," she said.

I smiled. "You look the same." We hadn't seen each other since college and she really did look the same. She was wearing a tight red dress and black heels. To the library.

"Are you busy? Do you want to go for a cup of coffee?" Leah asked.

"That sounds great," I said.

I followed her out of the library and around the corner to the Starbucks where we ordered boring, regular coffees and were lucky enough to find seats in the back.

"So, are you living in the city?" Leah asked and crossed her short legs.

"I'm staying with my friend, Ruby."

"Childhood friend?"

"Yes." Her memory still amazed me. When we sang together she was able to read a sheet of music only once before performing it perfectly.

"She was funny. I live with my girlfriend a few blocks from here."

"What?" In college Leah was a little too friendly with the men. And I do mean men, not boys, as she had an affinity for professors.

Leah gave me a little wink. "I know, I know, you never would've guessed it."

"Definitely not."

"Her name's Kate. You'll have to meet her some time."

"I might be moving to the city soon," I said, rubbing my hand against my jeaned leg to keep from scratching.

"By yourself?"

I nodded.

"Whatever happened with Adam?"

"I'm leaving him," I said and sipped my coffee.

"So you did marry him! Stupid girl," she said and smiled.

"I know. But I got three beautiful children out of the deal."

"That's great. Are they in the city, too?"

"No, the youngest two live in Boston, actually," I said and paused. Leah and I hadn't seen each other in thirty-something years and I was about to tell her my daughter was dead. I didn't know if it was too much to reveal but I was going to anyway. "My oldest passed away recently. Car accident."

"Oh, Janie, I'm so sorry," Leah said.

I wanted to shrug but feared that would be misunderstood. "She was a good kid," I said.

"I'm sure she was." Leah shifted in her seat and drank her coffee. Her eyes darted around the room. I'd made her uncomfortable.

I changed the subject and we chatted about the weather, our parents. Then she got to the meat of it.

"Are you still singing?" she asked.

My laugh was so bitter it was unrecognizable. "Not in a long time."

"Really? But you have the most beautiful voice."

"Don't be ridiculous," I said.

"Okay, I'm not even going to argue with you about this," Leah said and picked her purse up off the ground. She pulled out a piece of paper and a pen and smiled at me. "I want you to promise to audition for the Jewish People's Philharmonic Chorus." She scribbled some things down and dropped the paper in my lap.

"Absolutely not," I said without a smile. It had been too long, I was too out of practice.

Leah stared until I squirmed. "I'll hunt you down if you don't," she said.

I believed her. "Okay, okay. I'll give them a call."

"Good." She drained her coffee cup.

"Do you have to go?" I asked.

She nodded and stood, a huge smile on her face. "Come on," she said and motioned for me to stand.

I did. We hugged.

"Okay, please give me a call. I'm sorry I'm leaving in such a hurry— have to grab this book for Kate and then meet her at the apartment for some afternoon delight!" She disappeared out the door.

Chapter 9

Ruby was fixing us margaritas, complete with salted rim, as I got ready for my date with Rick. I was starting to enjoy myself more. I had the company of my two dogs and my best friend, plus Madison, Ruby's daughter, came around often. Madison was the same age as Nira. Seeing her hurt deep, like clothing that rubbed against an open wound. A constant reminder of the daughter I now lacked.

I heard the front door open as I finished combing my hair. I zipped up the sweat suit I'd put on after my shower, secured my hair in a towel, and made my way into the foyer to find Madison entering the apartment while balancing a large pizza. I held the door open for her.

"Thanks, Janie," she said and squeezed past me and into the kitchen. I followed, but lingered right outside the kitchen. "I got anchovies," Madison announced, placing the pizza on the counter.

"My favorite." Ruby appeared out of nowhere and gave her daughter a hug. The apartment wasn't big but the open layout could be deceiving. "I didn't expect you tonight."

"I wanted to see how you guys were doing," Madison responded.

I let out a gush of air. "I'm getting ready to go on a date with Rick."

"Finally!" Madison said and pulled plates and napkins from the appropriate cabinets. Everything in Ruby's apartment was located where it belonged—the exact opposite of my own home. I envied the neatness and order in Ruby's life. Madison hummed as she set the table in the eat-in kitchen.

Ruby sat while Madison finished getting everything out. "It's been a long time coming," Ruby said.

"You're both ridiculous," I said, still standing by the door of the kitchen.

"We're not the ones who are ridiculous," Ruby said, being mean. She still had to get in the occasional dig because I'd stayed with Adam for as long as I did. She divorced her own husband years ago simply because she didn't love him anymore. Nothing to do with words that cut like knives.

Madison ignored us. "Do you want some?" she asked me.

"No, thanks. Too nervous and I need to save my appetite for dinner."

She shrugged and dropped the pizza box in front of her mother. "Dig in," she said, taking a seat and helping herself to a slice. She bit into the pizza. "How are Sarah and Eric?" she asked.

"They're good. Sarah's not speaking to me," I said.

Ruby served herself.

"She throw a fit when you told her you were divorcing Adam?" Madison said.

"Naturally."

"She'll get over it," she said with her mouth full.

Ruby gave her daughter a dirty look.

"I meant because if I could deal with you and Dad getting divorced then Sarah can deal."

"I know what you meant," Ruby said. "I'd prefer you not say it with a mouthful."

"Sorry, sorry." Madison took another bite and wiped her face with a napkin. She gave her mother a big grin.

Ruby pretended to slap Madison. "Messy girl."

I glanced at the clock and my stomach flipped. I had less than thirty minutes to get ready. "I better get dressed," I said, my voice pitchy in panic.

I hurried off to Ruby's spare bedroom, my temporary home. Before my shower Ruby had helped me pick out my outfit. I hadn't been able to eat much lately. I was shedding pounds faster than I could keep up my wardrobe so the options we had to work with were limited. Ruby chose a black top that had flared sleeves and was tapered at the waist—something I didn't used to feel comfortable in, but now, well, now I looked pretty damn good. I picked my new black slacks and black flats to match. I was never a fan of heels, even though I was barely 5'2". I threw on gold hoop earrings, ran some mousse in my hair, and stared at my reflection in the mirror. I didn't recognize myself. I appeared younger and older at the same time. Familiar worry lines had softened, but my face was more defined because of the weight loss.

There was a knock at the door and Ruby poked her head in. "You should get going if you don't want to be late," she said.

I smiled. "I've never been late a day in my life."

"Well, then now wouldn't be a good time to start." She pushed the door the rest of the way open. "You look beautiful. Do you even have on make-up?"

"I forgot my make-up!" My short-lived calm facade had been broken. I ripped open my purse and pulled out the eye shadow. I proceeded to rush through the make-up process, a skill I developed while my children were infants.

Ruby laughed at me the whole time. "Well done," she said when I finished. She gave me a hug. "You're going to have so much fun tonight."

"You think so?" I wasn't so sure. I actually thought I might throw up on myself.

"Yes," she said and nodded with enthusiasm. "Positive."

I put all the make-up back into my purse and we walked to the front door.

"She's leaving!" Ruby called out to Madison, who came running into the room.

Madison clapped her hands together like a little girl. "You look so pretty!" she cried. Then her face fell. "Nira would be really happy for you."

Ruby glared at Madison.

It was true. And I had been avoiding that very thought all day. I knew Nira would be proud of everything I had done so far. But I didn't want to think about that right now.

"It's okay," I said, trying to re-lift everyone's spirits. I gave each of them a hug. "I won't be home too late."

"Don't make promises you can't keep," Madison said with a giggle.

Ruby laughed. "Yeah, I'm not going to wait up for you."

I frowned, but was trying not to laugh. I wished I was going to get lucky. Maybe I would. Without another word I spun around and walked out to my car; we were each taking our own because Rick was heading to the restaurant straight from work.

I drove in silence. I didn't want music flooding me with any more emotions than I was already dealing with. When I arrived at the restaurant I was shaking. I didn't know what car Rick drove so I had no way of telling if he was there already. I took a deep breath and got out of the car. Locking it was difficult with my trembling hands.

The restaurant was beautiful. I should have worn a skirt or dress. The lights, chandeliers encrusted in diamonds, were dim and hung close to the tables. Wallpaper, curtains, and chairs were adorned in red and gold. The freaking maître d' wore a tuxedo.

"Can I help you?" he asked. I'm pretty sure he was judging me.

"I'm joining someone. Rick Wilson."

"Ah, yes, Mr. Wilson," the maître d' said and warmed up to me. "He is waiting at the bar. I'll go get him."

The bar was just past the maître d' stand. I spotted Rick seated at the end, head bowed, in deep conversation with a young, trim redhead. Maybe I had been wrong in coming out. Maybe I should turn around and leave now, leave him to enjoy himself with the redhead. The host tapped Rick on the shoulder and all three looked over at me. I offered a weak smile. Rick said something to the woman and then walked toward me.

"Janie," he said. "I'm so glad you came."

Was he? "Thanks," I said. We hugged. It was awkward. I was awkward.

The maître d' joined us and escorted us to a table. It was a cozy table for two located in the back of the restaurant by a window. It was more romantic than any table I'd sat at with Adam.

We sat down. Me clumsily. The maître d' handed us our menus and wandered off, leaving me alone with Rick.

"You look great," Rick said.

I blushed. I couldn't help it. "Thank you."

"Should I order a bottle of wine?"

I nodded. Yeah, for me. I could drink several bottles.

A waitress walked by and Rick snapped his fingers at her. I chewed my lip. I didn't remember him being so uncouth.

"Can we see your wine list?" Rick said.

The waitress, probably still recovering from Rick summoning her with the snap of his fingers, didn't even offer us a smile. "I'll bring that over right away, sir," she said and twirled around. If she could've kicked dirt in our faces when she walked away she would have.

"So," Rick said and reached across the table, taking my hands in his. "How are you coping?"

"I'm fine," I said. "Ruby has been very supportive."

"Good, good," he said. "I always thought she was kind of a bitch."

"She is," I said.

He laughed and dropped my hands to the table. Leaning back in his chair, he ogled a different waitress at she walked by.

I was tempted to offer him a napkin to wipe away any drool. "How are you doing?"

"Oh, pretty great. Work is booming and the kids are all doing well— the oldest just got her PhD."

We both avoided bringing up our dissolved marriages.

"You must be proud," I said and smiled. "I'm actually thinking of applying to graduate school myself." I had only shared that with Ruby and Elsa so far.

"Really? What do you plan to study?" He seemed surprised.

"Same as my bachelors—special education," I answered.

"That's gutsy after all these years."

I laughed. "You think so?"

"Sure. I don't think everyone could do that at our age."

"So it's a bad idea because I'm ancient?" I'm sure Rick had a hard time telling if I was pissed off or not, because even I couldn't decide.

"We're both ancient," he said.

The waitress reappeared and propped the wine list in front of Rick. He scanned the menu and tapped at his choice on the list.

"Are you ready to order dinner?" she asked.

"Yes, we're ready," Rick said.

I hadn't even looked at the menu yet.

Rick proceeded to order calamari, Caesar salads, and shrimp fra diavlo for both of us. They were all things I liked, but I was put off by him ordering for me. I didn't remember him ever doing that before. The waitress wrote everything down and walked away. Rick watched.

This was who I'd been mooning over all these years? He had a poor sense of humor and in the short time we'd been dining together I'd witnessed him check out three different women. When we were teenagers I always felt like he had eyes only for me. Even when people were telling me he was fooling around with other girls.

I stared at my fingernails to avoid conversation.

Rick returned his attention to me. Sort of. "Did I tell you I might be purchasing a house in California?

"No, you didn't," I answered, already bored.

"Yes. The land surrounding it is several acres."

"Do you plan on moving?"

"No, don't worry," he said with a disgustingly sly smile.

The only thing I was worried about was not kicking that smile off his face with my new shoes.

The waitress was back quickly with two glasses and a bottle of wine. She poured Rick a taste first so he could sample it. He nodded and she poured me a glass as well, placed the bottle on the table, and hurried away.

Rick smiled. I squirmed in my seat. This was more awkward than our first date a million years ago. Back then it was okay to let your emotions and hormones take over, although I was usually able to keep them reigned in. I wasn't a typical teenager since I spent most of my time shielding Gabriella and Elsa from our parent's drama. But Gabriella, she was all hormones. All hot and bothered.

*

Gabriella was the beautiful one. Elsa and I never even had a chance to compete. I had the darkest skin and Elsa was almost clear, but Gabriella's skin was a perfect olive tone. The three of us didn't look related. People knew Gabriella because of her beauty and Elsa because of her personality. I was an ugly wallflower.

Rick was also beautiful. He had shaggy sandy brown hair that fell to his shoulders. It was a messier look than Farrah Fawcett's. I couldn't understand how I had been lucky enough to land him as my boyfriend. Elsa idolized him. When he came over she wanted him to play games with her, to be her older brother. Sometimes he humored her. But more often than not, it was just the two of us. Or so I thought. Elsa was ten but learned early on in her life how best to spy on Gabriella, aged fifteen, and me, aged seventeen. I never gave Elsa much ammunition, as I was a good girl, but Gabriella provided Elsa with more juicy gossip than she could swallow.

Rick and I were seated on the front steps of my parents' house. I was trying to check him out without him noticing and he was deep in thought. Elsa came running around the side of the house at full speed and collapsed in front of us.

"Hi Ricky!" she exclaimed. She was the only one he let call him that.

"Hi Elsa bear," he said and gave her a gentle nudge in the side with his foot. She giggled.

"Are you going out with Janie or Gabby tonight?" she asked.

I felt the blood rush out of my face and my hands grow cold. "What?" I stared at Rick, who avoided my eyes.

"Why are you so silly, Elsa bear?" he asked.

Elsa tilted her head to the side. "I'm not being silly. Sometimes you're with Janie and sometimes you're with Gabby. I'm just curious, is all."

I was still staring at Rick. "When are you with Gabriella?" I asked.

"I don't know what she's talking about," Rick said. "Curiosity killed the cat, Elsa." He stood and kicked some rocks around. He was trying to distract me and was failing.

Elsa, maybe sensing the tension, skipped away and into the house.

"Rick," I said. "What was Elsa talking about?"

He shook his head and shot me a grin—one that usually made my hands sweat. "Nonsense."

I climbed the stairs into the house with Rick at my heels. "Gabriella!" I called to the second floor.

She came down the stairs, skipping every other one. "What's up?" she said and smiled at Rick. "Hey Rick."

The way she said his name made me want to vomit. He was mine.

"Hi," he said and smiled at her. Oh, God.

Elsa joined us in the front hall.

"Elsa," I said. "Repeat what you said outside."

"What? That Rick and Gabby have dates together? They do, right? I heard Gabby talking about it on the phone."

"Yes, that'd be it," I said and glared at Gabriella. "What is she talking about, Gab?"

Gabriella shrugged. But not before catching Rick's eye. "No idea. She's being Elsa."

"What does that mean?" Elsa asked. "That I'm a liar? I'm not!" she ran out of the room, presumably to find our mother so she could tattle.

I crossed my arms and looked from Rick to Gabriella. I wasn't sure who to trust. Elsa was a pathological liar and Gabriella had trouble keeping her legs closed.

"What's going on?" I asked.

Rick shook his head. "Nothing's going on, Janie. Relax. Everything's cool." He smiled.

I wanted to wipe that smug smile off his pretty face. But I didn't. I never received a straight answer from either of them. And I let it go. Like I let everything go. Right then I started the pattern that set me up for failure for the rest of my life.

When the check came Rick grabbed it off the table. He wore a huge smile. Like he was proud of himself for picking up the check. I had money now. I could pay, too. But I didn't offer. The date was so bad I figured he deserved to pay. After he paid he walked me out to my car.

"That was fun," he said.

I nodded, pretending to agree.

Rick leaned against my car. The way he stood, the way he smiled—everything about him was cocky. How did I never notice that before? "When can we do this again?"

I was trying to think of a comeback that could maintain our friendship but put an end to anything romantic when an unfamiliar voice called my name. Rick stood up straight and the both of us turned back toward the restaurant.

"Plain Jane!" A stick of a woman said. She was tall and thin—half my weight. I didn't recognize her.

I offered a weak smile and tried to remember who the hell she was. Rick stared.

"It's Francine Banks!"

I wished she would stop exclaiming everything. But the name did ring a bell. "How's it going?" I asked.

She was right in front of us now. "You still don't remember me, do you?" She looked at Rick and back at me, her eyes wide. "We went to college together. Me, you, Adam, and Ted!" Now I remembered her. She was the annoying former girlfriend of Ted, one of Adam's old wrestling buddies. Sometimes I avoided matches so I wouldn't have to hear her headache inducing voice. She always wanted to chat—about nothing.

"Of course I remember you," I said. "I'll tell Adam you said hi." I wouldn't, but I wanted to wrap up the conversation.

Francine smiled. She had oversized teeth, like a horse. "Maybe I'll give him a call. It's been a while since we chatted." I was sure Adam wouldn't be excited about that phone call. He liked to chat, to gossip like an old lady, but even he'd found her irritating.

I nodded. "Sounds good." I saw Rick trying to hold back laughter.

"Well, I better go back inside and join the hubby," she said and giggled. She tried to offer me a hug, but it turned into more of a manly chest bump. "Ta-ta," she said and waved as she turned her back on us and returned to the restaurant.

"Wow," Rick said.

"Yeah," I agreed.

"Anyway." Rick settled back against the car. "I think you were saying something about not being able to wait to see me again."

I laughed. He was chauvinistic yet still cute. But I wasn't going to go out with him again. "We'll talk later, okay?" I asked.

Rick pulled away from the car and leaned into me. Was he going to try to kiss me? Did he think the date went well?

I turned away as if to check my watch. "I should get going. I don't want to wake Ruby when I get home." I put my keys into the door and looked at Rick out of the corner of my eye.

"Yeah, sure, me too. I have to get home. Lots of stuff to work on."

I turned a little and offered a half hug. It's all I was willing to give him now. After the way he behaved tonight I had no doubt that he slept with Gabriella. Elsa had been right all these years. I didn't even care. I would've forgiven Gabriella in a heartbeat in order to have her back.

"I'll call you," he said. He wouldn't.

I got into my car and drove back to Ruby's. This time I turned the radio on, ready to accept an onslaught of emotions. I couldn't chalk the whole night up as a bust. I still felt liberated. Alive. Rick wasn't who he used to be—or maybe he was never who I wanted him to be. Either way, I had gone on my first date in forty-one years and survived.

As I pulled up to Ruby's building my cell phone rang. I put the car in park and hesitated. It was after 10:00 PM, which was typically too late for me to be getting a phone call. I fumbled with my purse and pulled out the phone. It was Adam. I wasn't sure what to do. I had no idea why he was calling, but it could be an emergency. I hit the "talk" button and put the phone up to my ear.

"Hello?" I said.

"How was he?" Adam roared. I had to pull the phone away in order to stop the throbbing that Adam's voice started when it hit my eardrums.

"What?"

"Rick. Is he better now than when you were kids?"

That was a stupid question. Adam knew I never slept with Rick. In fact, Adam was the only man I'd ever slept with. Words couldn't explain how I wished that weren't so.

"Are you there? Are you with him right now?" Adam demanded when I didn't answer.

"Adam, it's late. Can I help you with something?" I couldn't believe I'd been dumb enough to answer the phone in the first place.

"Are you fucking kidding me? Stop whoring around."

"I don't know what you're talking about. Not that it's any of your business, but I've only been on one date."

"Yes, I'm fully aware that you had a date with Rick Wilson tonight."

"How do you know that?" I couldn't help myself.

"Francine Banks called me to say she caught you having an affair. What the hell, Janie? Were you making out in public?"

Did she call him from the Goddamn restaurant? "I'm sorry that Francine bothered you, but, like I said, it's none of your business what I do."

"I'm coming over."

"What?" My heart started racing.

"You're mine, Janie. You can't be going on dates with other men. I'm on my way to Ruby's to pick you up."

"I'm not going anywhere with you. You can't come here."

"I'm coming and I'm taking you home with me," he said and hung up.

I stared at the phone. I stared at the front door to Ruby's building. Neither gave me the answers I needed. I hurried inside and rushed down the hallway to Ruby's bedroom—knocking once before letting myself in. She turned over onto her back and opened one eye.

"You're home, so the date couldn't have been that great," she said. Then she must've seen the distorted expression on my face because she sat up. "What's wrong?"

"Get dressed. We need to get out of here." I threw the sweats she had lying on a chair at her.

Ruby crawled out of bed and started dressing. "What the hell's going on?"

"I ran into someone on my date. An old classmate of mine and Adam's."

She widened her eyes.

I nodded. "I guess she called him immediately. He's livid and says he's on his way over."

Ruby stopped moving. "What? He's on his way here?"

"Yes. I'm so sorry. Maybe we should get out of here."

She finished dressing. "But do you really think he'll show up? I mean, Adam is pretty full of broken promises."

My heart slowed a little. Maybe she was right. Maybe he wouldn't even come. "Do we want to risk it?" I asked.

"I think it's more likely that he won't come."

I nodded. "Okay."

"I need some coffee," she said and wiped her eyes with the back of her hand.

I followed her into the kitchen and waited while she used one of those fancy coffee makers that produced a cup in mere seconds.

"You really married a winner," Ruby said and shook her head.

"I know, I know. I'm really sorry about all this, Ruby."

"Forget about it. You can't control his behavior." She picked her coffee cup up with both hands and took a slow sip. "Do you want one?"

"No, thanks. I'll never be able to sleep as it is."

We headed into the living room and sat on the couch. I was tense, solid stone. Ruby didn't seem much better.

I let out a deep breath.

"Forget about it," Ruby said again. "Tell me about your date with Rick."

I rolled my eyes.

"That bad?"

"That bad. He was much smoother when we were kids. Or at least I couldn't see through him back then." I laughed.

"What do you mean?"

"He was checking out every decent looking woman at the restaurant, including the waitress."

"Okay, so nothing's changed."

"Haha, very funny," I said. "But I guess not."

"Are you upset?"

"Well, yeah. I don't know. It was my first date in a long time. I didn't expect it to be such a bust."

"Understandable," Ruby said and tucked her legs underneath her. "Will you go out with him again?"

"Definitely not."

"Not even to get laid?" She smiled widely.

"Ah, that would be nice," I said.

"How long has it been?" She drank the last of her coffee and placed the mug on a coaster on the coffee table.

"Ruby!" I smacked her with a throw pillow.

"Come on, it's me."

"It's been too long, okay? And I would've loved to have slept with Rick."

"I know you would've, I just wanted to hear you say it," Ruby said and laughed hysterically, practically rolling around on the couch she was so pleased with herself.

"I'm not a born-again virgin, right?" I asked, only half joking.

Ruby composed herself. "Don't be stupid. I will make it my new mission in life to get you some amazing sex, how's that?"

"Sure. Go for it."

Ruby put the television on and we watched the news in silence. As the final report came to an end she looked at the clock. "Still no Adam."

"You're right," I said. I hadn't noticed the time passing.

"In the morning we should go to the police station."

"We should?" The thought never occurred to me.

"Jesus, Janie. You can't be living in fear. You should file a complaint about him harassing you."

"Can't my lawyer do that for me?"

"I don't know. Possibly."

"Will you come with me?"

Ruby stared at me as if I had two heads. "Of course."

"Okay, sure." Why not? I'd already filed for divorce and pressed charges against the love of my life for forgery. Why not add harassment to the mix?

I sank into the couch. Ruby must've done the same, because suddenly it was morning.

*

We went straight to the police station. I'd never been inside one before. Ruby stayed by my side the entire time. I knew there was a reason I kept her around all these years.

The policeman that greeted us defied stereotypes. He was fit and without a hint of a doughnut belly. His smile was warm. "How can I help you ladies tonight?" he asked in a sweet, relaxed voice.

"I need to file a complaint."

The policeman's face turned from friendly to serious. "Against who?"

"My husband. Well, soon to be ex-husband."

"Have you ever filed a complaint before?"

I shook my head. I could feel the sweat beading on my forehead and between my fingers, seeping into my palms.

"Okay. Do you want to file an order of protection?"

I looked at Ruby and she nodded. It's not that I thought it was the wrong thing to do, but I needed constant validation in my actions. I'd made enough mistakes on my own.

"Yes," I told the police officer.

"So let me tell you how this works. I can walk you through the paperwork to file a complaint. Then I want you to sign an agreement stating that you will go to the courthouse to file the order of protection."

I must've seemed as overwhelmed as I felt because he stopped talking.

"Why don't we take a seat?" he said and pointed to a lobby area.

The three of us sat down.

"I'm Officer Dargon by the way," he said and stuck out his hand.

He had a rough handshake, but it was reassuring. It might mean he knew what he was doing.

"I'm Janie and this is my friend Ruby," I said.

Officer Dargon and Ruby eyed one another. I envied the looks they exchanged. Made me wish things hadn't fallen through with Rick.

"You should go to Family or Criminal Court and ask the help desk for the Petition Room. You can either hire a lawyer or have the state appoint one, or not involve a lawyer at all, but they can help you file the restraining order. Once that has been completed and signed by the judge, the courthouse will send the official documentation back to the police station so that we can serve your husband."

I didn't realize it, but I was clenching Ruby's hand in my own. She squeezed back and whispered, "It'll be okay."

The officer handed me a clipboard with paperwork attached. It was a simple form asking not so simple questions about my relationship with Adam. I answered to the best of my ability. I didn't need Officer Dargon or Ruby's help with that. I was perfectly capable of summing up the difficulties in my life all on my own.

Ruby and the officer chit-chatted while I filled out the complaint form. I was lost in my own miserable world, but I got the impression they might end up going on a date. Where one relationship goes to die another begins.

Chapter 10

The courthouse was straight out of the movies. A stone staircase led up to gold-framed doors and massive glass windows. Several days had passed since my visit to the police station. It took that much time to gather up the courage to come to the courthouse. Ruby offered to take the day off from work to go with me but I told her she didn't have to. Now that I looked at the overbearing building and the ragged people entering it I wasn't so sure. At least my lawyer was supposed to meet me.

I walked by security and through the metal detectors. I never would've guessed that I'd end up in a place like this. I took a seat by the information desk and waited for Mr. Wrentham's arrival.

By the time Mr. Wrentham arrived I was riddled with anxiety. And questions. Was I doing the right thing? Was Adam so bad I needed to file a restraining order? I knew the answers even as I asked the questions.

"Hi Janie," Mr. Wrentham said and gave me a gentle hug. His warmth calmed me. "Follow me, we need to go to the Petition Room to fill out the appropriate paperwork."

I followed him in silence.

We entered the cold, bright room and Mr. Wrentham gathered the forms from the clerk.

He led me to a table in the corner and pulled a chair out for me. We were both seated.

"So, fill me in on what's been happening," Mr. Wrentham requested. He hadn't asked for much over the phone, promising he would get the details from me in person.

"I went to the police station and filed a complaint against my husband with an officer. He suggested that I come here to file an order of protection."

Mr. Wrentham nodded. "Is that what you want to do? I don't want you filing just because an officer told you to."

"Yes, this is what I want to do," I assured him.

"Okay. We'll complete the paperwork and then go into the courtroom to speak to the judge. If he approves the order, the court will send a copy to the police station that will then serve your husband. Make sense?"

I nodded. "The officer told me a little bit about the process."

We filled out the form together. It was similar to the complaint form, although more invasive. There were questions about Adam's car and license plate number so that the police could find him to serve him. My hand trembled when I wrote that information down. The most difficult task was writing about the various ways that Adam harassed and stalked me. I hesitated.

"Are you okay?" Mr. Wrentham asked. "Do you need to take a break?"

"No, I can do this." I wrote about Adam's behavior at Nira's will reading, his showing up at Ruby's apartment, and his threat to come and take me away. As I was writing I realized I didn't know any more if he wanted me or my money. It was like he and I had a threesome with money over the past thirty-two years. How depressing. I slid the completed form across the table.

"All set?" Mr. Wrentham said and scanned the form.

"As set as I'll ever be, I guess."

Mr. Wrentham nodded. "I'm going to pass this along to the clerk, who will draft the petition, and then we'll be called when it's time to head into the courtroom." He stood and smiled. "Everything will work out."

Waiting to be called into the courtroom was beyond nerve-racking. I ground my teeth into the gums. I couldn't help but think about the last time I almost ended up in a courthouse because of Adam. When he still pretended to be a decent father but was already a beast.

*

Sometimes Adam was good to our children. He coached each of them in one sport or another. It was with Sarah that picking on someone became one of Adam's specialties—especially over the summer she turned thirteen.

I took a deep breath and headed down the hall. The walls were littered with happy family photos. Pictures that told a false story.

When I walked into our bedroom, Adam was lying on the bed on top of the covers with the TV blasting. "Maybe you could let Sarah play the position she wants. I think she said pitcher." I crawled onto the bed next to him.

Adam muted the TV. He shifted on the bed to face me and gave me such a look of hatred my insides twitched. "Don't tell me what to do." He was grinding his teeth.

"She's just a kid, Adam."

He crossed his arms. "I know that."

"Please give her the same opportunity as the other kids."

"Janie. I said *don't tell me what to do*." His words were arrows that nicked my flesh with every angry pause.

"I'm sorry." Then I smelled the vodka on his breath. "Were you drinking at practice?"

Adam rolled his eyes in anger. At one point I glanced only white.

Sarah walked by then, wrapped tightly in a towel. She stood in the doorway and we made eye contact for one brief moment.

Suddenly Adam's fist rammed into my chin. Then I was flying through the air with a boom and a bang and blood in my eye. I hit my forehead on the nightstand before colliding with the hardwood floor. I heard a whimper and Sarah scurried away.

"Oh, Jesus, Janie, I'm sorry." Adam was at my side before I could stand. He kneeled next to me, rested his hand on my shoulder. "I'm so, so sorry."

I jerked away. "Leave me alone," I whispered. I rubbed my hip where it smashed into the ground. "Get the fuck away from me," I said through clenched teeth. Pulling up and away, I managed to prop myself against the bed without his help. I took a tissue from the end table and wiped the blood from my eye.

"So, so sorry." He was still close to me. I could feel the heat of the wound on my forehead at the same time I felt the heat from his body.

"Don't," I said with less strength.

"Baby," he said and tried to kiss my neck. I pulled away. He was a leper.

"No. No 'baby.'" I tried to push past him, to leave the room, but he grabbed my elbow.

"Please." Adam's voice dripped with honey. "I said I'm sorry. Let me make it up to you."

Make it up to me? I wanted to scream, to cry, to punch him in the face. I didn't want to love someone who would treat me like this.

He let go of my elbow to brush the hair from the cut above my eye. His hand was light like a bird, far lighter than when he knocked me off the bed. I still backed away.

Adam stared at me as I walked from the room. He didn't follow. I entered Sarah's room, where I found her changed into her pajamas and seated on the bed with clean, sparkly tears glittering her cheeks.

"I'm okay," I told her and grabbed her hand. "I'm okay, but I want you to come with me now." I did not want to stay in that house and I was not going to leave Sarah at Adam's mercy.

Sarah stood and I led her from her room and down the stairs. I instructed her to get on her coat and shoes while I ran around in circles until I found my car keys. Then we fled from that Godforsaken house. I wished it were for good.

"Where are we going?" Sarah asked as we climbed into my car.

I turned over the engine. "We're going to Aunt Gabriella's." Gabriella was single, unlike Elsa, and her home was the easiest place for me to escape to.

Sarah and I always had trouble connecting and drove the twenty minutes from Weston to Boston in silence. I didn't even give my sister a heads up. My head was foggy and I kept watching the black and white movie of what happened replay in my mind. Sarah was quiet and barely moved. I didn't know how to comfort her.

I pulled into the visitor parking lot at Gabriella's apartment building and turned off the car. I could feel Sarah watching me, waiting to see what would happen next.

"Come on." I got out of the car and waited.

Sarah came and stood next to me. Still silent—more silent than she'd ever been in her life.

I again took her hand and we walked together to the front door. I rang the bell for Gabriella's apartment.

"Hello," she said, her voice pouring through the speaker.

"It's Janie and Sarah."

My sister buzzed us in. She lived on the fourth floor and there was no elevator.

"I'm too tired," Sarah said as we stared at the staircase before us.

"I know, but you can go to sleep as soon as we get upstairs." I didn't wait for an answer and started to climb the stairs with Sarah's hand still wrapped in mine, dragging her behind me.

She groaned a bit, but otherwise stayed quiet. When we arrived on the fourth floor. Gabriella stood there waiting for us with open arms. Literally. We made eye contact and exchanged words in silence that only a sister would understand. She pulled Sarah toward her, embracing her in a full body hug.

We went inside and Gabriella double-bolted the door behind us.

"Why don't you go lay down in Auntie's guest room?" I gave Sarah a gentle push and she ran off.

Gabriella and I sat on the couch and looked at each other.

"What happened?" she said and reached forward to touch the wound on my face.

"I don't even know, Gab." I started to cry. Real, round, bulbous tears that blinded my vision and soaked my cheeks.

"Well, your face knows. Did Adam hit you?" Gabriella had been there before. Over the years she'd had a string of abusive boyfriends. Many of them were in jail now—for a variety of things, none of which were a result of Gabriella pressing charges, because she never did. She was small, although not as tiny as Elsa, and didn't seem to mind getting pushed around.

"He shoved me off the bed."

"In front of Sarah?" She didn't wait for a response and punched the throw pillow. "That son of a bitch."

I sniffled. "What do I do?"

Gabriella frowned. "Nothing. It's not worth it."

I'd never asked Gabriella for advice before. Even through all the times I fled to her apartment to get away from Adam's screaming. She was the middle sister, the troublemaker. She ran around and did her thing and didn't bother much with anyone else and what they thought. And when her boyfriends' beat her she let them and continued to love them. I'd never asked her for advice before for the obvious reasons. Now I didn't know what else to do. I refused to put this burden on Elsa, as she was already dealing with a cheating husband.

"I can't do nothing, can I? I can't have Sarah witness something like that again. Thank God Nira and Eric weren't around."

"Look, you remember Jeremy?"

Jeremy was one of her college boyfriends. I remembered him because she dated him around the time that Adam and I started seeing each other. There were a lot of double dates. There'd also been Adam's absurd suspicion that Jeremy and I were sleeping together. I nodded.

"He was the first guy to ever lay a hand on me. I took it seriously. I went to the police. I don't know if it was because it was the '70s or because the cop was an asshole, but he explained how the court system worked. And it didn't sound good. It seemed like a whole lot more work than I was willing to put forth, all because my boyfriend took a swing at me and clipped my ear."

"But Adam isn't my boyfriend, Gab, he's my husband. And there are children involved."

"All the more reason to forgive and forget. He's never done this before, right?"

I nodded. Thankful.

"Why don't we sleep on it?" Gabriella suggested.

I nodded. "You're right. Things will seem clearer in the morning." I wrapped my arms around her. She smelled like hairspray, always did. I was comforted by the familiar smell and took a deep breath.

The next morning we didn't say another word about it. I wasn't going to go to the police. I don't know if Sarah ever told her brother and sister, but they never mentioned it to me. That was the one time Adam laid a hand on me. And a big reason I never left him was that he didn't do it again.

*

When there was finally a knock on the conference room door I nearly jumped out of my skin. Mr. Wrentham and I walked together into the courtroom. We sat on hard wooden chairs to the right of the judge's bench. I was gnawing my nails down to the wicks.

"All rise," an officer said.

We stood.

"You may be seated."

We sat. The officer called me up to the witness stand and swore me in. I was drenched in sweat. My head was pounding.

The judge was a white, hairy, obese old man. He looked like Santa Claus.

"Hello Mrs. Brown," he greeted me.

I nodded, since my mouth was dry and my tongue was frozen.

"Mr. Wrentham is representing you?"

"Yes, sir," I responded.

He read over the petition. "Is everything here true and accurate?" he asked.

"Yes," I said.

"Do you currently have any other charges against your husband?"

I looked at Mr. Wrentham, unsure of how to answer.

"Mr. Wrentham?" the judge asked.

Mr. Wrentham stood. "Yes, your honor, we've filed for divorce and are in the process of filing charges for forgery."

The judge nodded and motioned for Mr. Wrentham to sit down before turning back to me. "Has your husband ever physically abused you?"

"He pushed me once."

"Have you ever been physical with him?"

I hung my head in shame, like a dog that got caught crapping behind the couch. "Yes," I mumbled.

The judge sighed. "Do you feel that your life will be in danger if you don't receive this order of protection?"

"Yes, I do," I said. I really did. What did Adam have left to lose? He had no money, no one left in the house to abuse. He may as well come after me.

"I am going to issue a temporary order of protection and a summons to serve your husband. The order of protection will be good for twenty days, at which time you will have to return if you wish to file a permanent restraining order. Do you understand these terms?"

"Yes," I said.

The judge shuffled papers around, scribbled down his signature, and dismissed me.

When we stepped outside the courtroom Mr. Wrentham grinned. "This is good," he said. "This is a step in the right direction. It shouldn't be long before Adam is served and we should be able to charge him with forgery soon. I'm also in the process of setting up the preliminary conference for your divorce."

I didn't have freedom yet, but the familiar taste lingered on my tongue from decades earlier.

Chapter 11

I followed through with Leah's demands and called the Jewish People's Philharmonic Chorus for an audition. I missed singing too much not to. They asked me to come in right away, yet I was reluctant. I couldn't remember my last audition. My throat was hoarse, my forehead hot.

I succumbed to public transportation and left my car behind. My breath was whisked away by the architecture of the building. It was an old hotel that had been converted into apartments a couple of blocks from the Hudson River. The building had everything—stone, brick and iron, and elaborate pillars and columns. I walked through glass doors into a lobby that was much simpler than the outside of the building dictated. The carpet was brown and worn. The wallpaper, probably once bright and welcoming, was dull and the colors all blended together.

Before I knew it a small, elderly woman was at my side.

"Mrs. Freedman?" she asked.

"Yes, I'm Ms. Janie Freedman."

She clapped her hands together. "Welcome! My name is Rona. I'm so happy you've come to audition for the Jewish People's Philharmonic Chorus. We're honored to hear you sing."

I was flattered. "Thank you. I'm happy to be here."

"Follow me," she said, turning on her heels.

I followed her down a short hallway and into a large room. There were five people, three men and two women, seated in a row with music stands in front of them. This was it. I took a deep breath. "Hello," I said from the doorway, not at all demonstrating the power of my voice.

"Hello and welcome," one of the women said. They went from left to right announcing their names, each of them wearing a smile. A creepily friendly group.

Rona still stood by the door. "Let me take your purse," she said.

I slid the bag off my shoulder and handed it to her. Aside from that action I was motionless, boneless. A piece of spaghetti.

"We'd like you to sing the piece of your choice—acapella," Rona said.

Well, that wouldn't be challenging at all.

She pointed to an X marked in red tape several feet in front of the row of people.

With great pain and hesitation, I walked over to the X and stood before the group. I wished I wasn't so out of practice, that Adam hadn't made me stop singing in the first place. I'd even stopped singing in the shower. I shook my head. Singing was another thing I should've fought harder for.

*

If people argued in musical tones it would be so much sweeter. I could hear Adam and Sarah yelling at each other in the living room and tried to ignore it. Nira was staying after school to work on the senior play. Hopefully she would be home soon to silence the animals upstairs and put them in their place. I opened my mouth wide and continued with my "Do-Re-Mi..." It was time for the High Holidays and the Jewish Community Center put on a concert every year. It was the one moment when all eyes were on me and I didn't mind.

When we bought the house in Weston years ago the basement had already been refinished. I took it upon myself to make it into a little music studio. Paintings and posters of my favorite singers lined the walls. The biggest, most colorful was a painting of Bette Midler that Nira won off an eBay auction. I draped a sheer red curtain over the single window so that it was as if a constant bloody sunset streamed into the room.

I tried to forget about the noisy family upstairs in order to sing to my heart's content. Too late. Sarah came stumbling down the basement stairs with Eric at her heels. I stopped mid "La" and waited for one of them to speak.

"Dad wants to know when dinner is," Sarah said.

If she'd asked for her or Eric I wouldn't have minded. But Adam was a grown man. He couldn't ask himself? He couldn't fix something to eat? The glow I received from singing faded.

I tidied up the sheets of music on the stand before turning to my children. They looked at me with their round cheeks and messy hair, having only recently returned from a baseball game with friends at the park.

"Are you hungry?" I asked.

Eric nodded.

"Yeahhh, duh," Sarah replied.

"Okay, I'll make you kids some macaroni and cheese." It was their favorite and Adam usually didn't mind it.

The three of us trudged up the stairs and into the kitchen. Eric situated himself at the counter. He crossed his arms and rested his head while Sarah helped me. Making macaroni and cheese from a box wasn't difficult, but Sarah had a love for cooking and participated whenever she could.

Adam entered the kitchen, his presence emanating tension.

Eric lifted his head, saw his father, and walked out of the room.

Something must've happened between them earlier. Something was always happening between Adam and someone.

I ignored Adam and pulled the milk and butter from the refrigerator. Adam was in such a rush, always was, to get at his beer that he bumped into me and the milk almost went flying.

"What are you making?" he asked.

"Mac and cheese," Sarah said, the happiness stretched across her face.

"Ugh," Adam spat, revolted. "I hate that shit."

I tried not to shrug. "It's what the children wanted."

"Do the children pay the bills?"

Sarah pulled the pot from the cabinet and handed it to me with a weak smile, her earlier happiness already diminished.

I ran the pot under the water and then set it on the stove.

"Janie," Adam said.

I turned the stove on and turned toward him. "What?"

Sarah pulled the pasta strainer from the counter and placed it in the sink.

"Do the children pay the bills?" Adam repeated.

"No, obviously not," I said. The patch on my arm began to itch.

Adam put his mug down on the counter with a loud thud. "Don't be rude. I've been listening to you practice singing. You're terrible. And since money is so tight I'm canceling membership at the JCC."

I leaned against the counter. "What?"

"You heard me. No more singing."

Without looking at me Sarah left the room. Left me to Adam.

"I have to sing," I said. "Let me get a job to pay for the JCC."

Adam mashed his lips together and exhaled loudly through his nose. "Not happening. I haven't paid this month yet, so they probably won't let you perform in the High Holidays play." He turned to leave the room.

I picked up his beer mug and whipped it at him. The glass hit him in the back of the head and crashed to the ground. At first I was proud. But then it took Adam forever to turn around.

He opened his mouth wide and leaned against the counter. And howled.

I bit my lip. What had I done? "Are you okay?" I asked.

Adam put his hand up to the back of his head. When he pulled it away I saw the blood on his hand. He collapsed to the ground.

Oh, God. This couldn't be happening. I rushed to his side. He was out cold and there was blood draining from the back of his head onto the grayish-green tiles, seeping into the grout. There was a soft whimper behind me and I turned to find Sarah in the doorway of the kitchen.

"Baby," I said.

Her eyes opened wide.

"Can you dial 911? Tell them we need an ambulance?" Why wasn't Nira home yet? I couldn't drive Adam to the hospital with Sarah and Eric in tow.

She nodded and grabbed the phone from its cradle, dialing with shaky hands.

Adam still didn't move.

"Eric!" I yelled.

Sarah shushed me and walked out of the room, talking quietly into the phone.

"What?" Eric yelled back.

"Get downstairs with some towels. Quickly!" I prayed that for once he did what he was told without hesitation.

Moments later Eric appeared with two large blue towels. I placed one under Adam's head and wiped up some of the blood with the other. The towel, saturated with blood, turned purple.

Eric didn't say anything. He stood in the corner and watched me cradle his father.

Sarah came back into the room. "They said less than ten minutes," she said.

"What?" Eric asked.

"An ambulance. Your sister called an ambulance," I said. I stared, amazed, at the blood that continued to flow from Adam's head.

"What did you do to Dad?" Eric asked.

"I didn't do anything. It was an accident," I said. But it wasn't. I hadn't accidentally thrown the mug at Adam.

"Was it his fault?" Sarah asked. "Did he hurt you first?"

I didn't know how to answer that. I'd been hurting for years. I shook my head.

It was less than five minutes before the ambulance arrived at the house. None of us moved during that time. I lost myself staring at Adam, at the years behind us, at what led us to this point.

The doorbell rang and I jumped. "Let them in," I told Eric.

He ran from the room and to the front door. Then the kitchen was a crime scene. Two EMT's knelt beside Adam. One checked his pulse and the other wrapped gauze around his head.

"What happened?" One asked.

"I threw a glass at him." I was too shocked to lie.

He nodded. "There's been a lot of blood loss. Phil, you ready?" Together they hoisted Adam's large body onto a stretcher.

"Will you be riding in the ambulance or following us?" The one named Phil asked.

I looked at Sarah and Eric. They were still frozen. "I'll have to come later, after my oldest gets home and can watch them," I said to Phil.

The EMT's carried Adam outside and loaded him into the ambulance, like old luggage.

Nira pulled into the driveway as the ambulance pulled away.

*

I opened my mouth and the music flowed out like liquid. I sounded beautiful, even to me. At first I tried not to make eye contact with the judges, but then I was about to burst with confidence so I looked at each one of them. They still wore their smiles.

I'd chosen to sing *I Will Survive* by Gloria Gaynor. I could be cliché once in a while. I wished my children were there to hear me. They'd always loved my singing. They were my biggest fans. I closed my eyes and imagined a great, big audience spread out before me, cheering me on.

When I finished the song the smiling people stood and applauded. I'd been out of practice, but maybe singing was like getting back on a bicycle.

Rona took my hand in hers and glanced at the row of judges. They nodded.

"We'd be fools not to ask you to join us," Rona said.

"Please say you'll start coming to rehearsals," one of the other women added.

I wouldn't have said no for another half million dollars.

Chapter 12

I couldn't remember the last time I lived alone. I'm pretty sure the realtor was judging me for being elderly and looking for my own apartment in the city. The one thing about gaining independence so late in life is having to accept that everyone thinks you're already near death.

The realtor was younger than Eric and Sarah. She reminded me of the model Twiggy. And of how much I hated that model while growing up. Did she eat twigs for breakfast? She had the same short, pixie cut and her name was Melody. Her voice was melodious. She strummed her pointy red nails across the desk. We were seated in her pristine white office in the Upper West Side, not too far from where the auditions for the chorus had been held. There was so much white in the room it felt like an insane asylum.

"Now, Mrs. Freedman—"

"Ms. Freedman," I corrected her.

"Sorry," she said. "On the phone you said you're looking for short-term rental possibilities in this area?" It was as if she sang every word.

"Yes," I said. "Two bedroom." I wanted a spare room in case Eric came to visit or Sarah ever started talking to me again. I wanted a place my sister could escape to, just as she had offered me such a space all these years. I gave Melody a price range that Eric told me was reasonable, since I had no idea.

Melody stared at me, as if trying to understand what I was doing there. She was judging again. "Will anyone be cosigning the lease with you?"

"No, just me." Forever and always.

"Alright, I have a few places in mind that you might like. We can walk, the first one's very close to here," she said and stared at me with her big blue eyes.

"Sure, that sounds okay."

I followed her outside.

"It's a beautiful day," Melody said with a wide smile.

I nodded, nervous about viewing the first apartment.

Melody hummed while we walked, until we stopped short in front of a modern apartment building. Everything was made of marble and stone. It screamed royalty. And it had to be out of my budget, because even though I inherited more money than I was used to, I was still going to be smart about it.

"Breathtaking, isn't it?" Melody asked.

I nodded, too amazed to speak.

Melody giggled, showing her age. "Wait until you see inside," she said and stepped forward. I followed her through a rotating door into a shiny marble lobby. A round man somewhere in his thirties sat propped up behind the welcome desk.

"Hi Melody," he said, batting his eyes.

"Hi Stan," she said, musical as always.

"You look beautiful today." Stan smiled. His face was so fat that with the smile his eyes almost disappeared.

"Thank you. I'm going to take Janie here up to see 3B."

We rode an elevator up to the third floor. It had mirrors framed by crystals on every side. I prefer not to look at my reflection, but was too distracted by the beauty of the design to notice I was standing in front of myself.

Even the door to the apartment declared elegance. It was solid wood, covered in carved flowers, and made a heavy clunk when Melody closed it behind us.

I might have stopped breathing when I took my first look inside. The apartment was more than I could ever have hoped for. It was big, but not too big. I wouldn't kill myself keeping it clean. The appliances were all new and shiny—I could see my reflection everywhere. Melody gave me a tour from room to room, each one more amazing than the last. It even had an additional half bathroom.

"I don't understand," I said to Melody after we returned to the front of the apartment. "This apartment is too perfect. There has to be something wrong with it."

Melody laughed. "There isn't. The maintenance company that runs it is very nice and they are quick to respond to any issues. I suppose the only negative thing is that they don't reside on-site so it may take a bit longer for them to get over here at times."

"That's fine," I said.

"So, what are you thinking? Are you interested? Would you like to see more apartments? I have two or three others that you might like."

I didn't need to see another apartment. My mind was made up. "I want this one," I said.

Melody nodded. "I thought so. I saw the way your eyes lit up when we got inside and I knew."

I don't think my eyes ever lit up before, so that must make this meant to be. Melody promised to call me as soon as she heard something from the landlord. We parted ways and I headed back to Ruby's, high from excitement.

The next morning I was awoken by the cell phone.

"Hi, Mrs.—Ms.—Janie? I'm calling with some bad news." It was Melody.

"Already?" I was used to bad news, but didn't expect it to happen so soon. Bad news liked to take its time, like the opposite of when you yank off a bandage.

"The management company for the apartment you're interested in is very efficient. Unfortunately, they ran a credit report and I'm afraid you'll need a cosigner if you still want the apartment."

My heart thudded so hard against my chest that even my head shook. My credit was that bad? Adam destroyed it that much? I had no idea how to fix it. Sounded like another reason to meet with my lawyer. Or hire a hitman—since I had the money, why dirty my own hands?

"Hello?" Melody said. I guess I took too long answering, too long pondering how to kill off Adam.

"Yes, sorry. I'm a little surprised is all." I shouldn't have been.

"Is there someone that could cosign with you or should we look at some more apartments?"

I didn't want other apartments, I wanted that one. It was perfect for me. I was already willing to call it home. And somehow, someway, it was within my price range. "I think I can find someone," I said. I wasn't sure who, but I had options. I had a sister and a best friend who would do anything for me. Time to call in another favor.

*

I suppose my family wasn't so bad, after all. It wasn't difficult to convince Elsa to cosign for the apartment with me. Now I was eating brunch with my son at a small café near my new home. We were seated at a tiny table cramped into the corner by the front window. I liked it because we could watch the different characters that made up New York wander by.

Eric had been kind enough to offer help in moving my old life to my new apartment. He had gone so far as to contact Adam to set up a date when he wouldn't be home to harass us. Eric and I were efficient in packing up my things and managed to avoid Adam altogether. I think I held my breath the entire time.

"You look good," Eric said. I wished Sarah could've seen, too, but she still refused to talk to me. Instead of losing one daughter I'd lost two.

"Thanks," I said and took a sip of my mimosa. I moved the scrambled eggs around on my plate with my fork and nibbled at my toast.

"Have you been working out?" Eric asked.

I laughed. "No. I haven't been eating much."

"Well, that's not healthy," he said.

"I know that, honey, but I haven't had much of an appetite. I'm going to join a gym by the new apartment."

"Good. It'll be good for you." He was sounding wiser than he used to.

"Do you think Sarah will visit my new apartment?"

Eric's face twitched a little, showing more emotion than usual. "I wouldn't count on it. She's been visiting Dad on the weekends."

"Really?" I felt my heart strings being twisted around a fork like they were spaghetti. It felt something like betrayal.

"He's still our dad," Eric said.

"I know." I stared at my eggs. They resembled mashed brains.

"He needs someone around and I don't have the time."

While Eric was situated, Sarah was still finding herself. It was hard to believe they shared my womb together. I guess while she figured out her own path she could spare time to devote to keeping her father alive. There was no doubt that if he were left in charge of himself someone would find him dead, a bloated fish on the couch.

"I know," I said again.

"Are you mad?" he asked. He never cared before.

"No. I don't think he deserves help, but that's Sarah's choice." I took another sip of my mimosa and felt the citrusy alcoholic beverage bounce around in my stomach. "How does she pay?" Traveling from Boston to Yonkers wasn't free.

Eric avoided eye contact. "I pay."

"Okay." I tensed my feet.

"He's a mess," Eric said.

"I'm sure he is."

"And he asks about you."

"What do you want me to say, Eric? This is hard for me, too."

Eric drank his water and wrinkled his brow.

"What? It's not hard for me?"

He put his glass on the table and water spilled over the edge. "I know it's hard for you, but it's harder for him because he's an idiot."

I laughed. "Don't call your father an idiot," I said. He smiled. I was always telling the children to respect their father, even when I didn't.

Chapter 13

The university was big. Otherworldly big. But after meeting with a new lawyer and dealing with the trust account I was up for anything. I stood in front of the giant glass doors and felt grateful to be there. The bustle of students was overwhelming, but intoxicating. Their youth gave me strength.

I entered the building but stopped short inside. I was in a massive hallway where hundreds of voices echoed. Before I could let my hesitation keep my feet rooted to the ground I plunged forward and followed the signs to the Admissions Office.

A man slightly older than me sat seated behind a long desk inside. He had a bitter, lopsided frown and yellow teeth. "Good Morning," he grunted. His voice was rougher than I expected, like new sandpaper against rusty metal.

"Hello," I said and tried to smile.

"Can I help you with something?" He was tense. I suspected he didn't really want to help. He walked over to an assortment of brochures spread out on a table to the left of the office door.

"I'm interested in enrolling in some classes and to possibly work toward a Master's degree," I said. I tried to hide the eagerness in my voice and failed, sounding more like a college freshman than a senior citizen.

"Have you looked at the class listings?"

I nodded. "I looked at them online." Before Nira died she made me sit down and learn various computer applications. It was like learning a different language. I never had any desire to use a computer, but because of my love for learning, Nira thought I should. She was right. I ran searches on everything from arachnophobia to Zumba.

"I have my Bachelor's in special education." I felt awkward and the man wasn't doing anything to help. "I was going to sign up for some classes that interest me and think about my Master's later. Is that not a good idea?"

"Sounds okay," he said and sat back behind his desk.

"Can I ask you something?" I felt I needed permission since he was so cold.

"Okay."

"Are there a lot of older students enrolled here? Students my age?" I'd hate to be the mother, or worse yet—grandmother, of the class.

"I guess there are some people over thirty."

That didn't quite comfort me.

"Wanna sit?" He asked and gestured to a small chair to the left of his desk.

"No, thank you," I said. I was too nervous to be confined to a chair. "I'm interested in continuing to pursue special education. But I haven't been in a classroom for a very long time."

He pulled back a little, as if offended that I didn't take a seat. "The school will prepare you for that." He stood and grabbed several more brochures and handed them to me. He sure loved those brochures. "You want to talk to one of our advisors some time? Or you can fill out the application and mail it in."

He might be right about suggesting I talk to a college advisor. Although, what I really needed was a life coach to lay out every step for me until the day I died. I was tired of making decisions. But at the same time I was eager to get back to school and study.

"Sure, I'd like to make an appointment with the advisor," I said.

He pulled out an appointment book and we scheduled a meeting for the next week. I hoped the advisor was nicer than this guy. I offered him one more smile and was once again denied.

I exited the school and was reminded of when Nira first went off to college. I'd been devastated. She moved into the dorms even though the school was twenty minutes from the house. Those twenty minutes felt like an eternity and the house was a rotting corpse without her.

*

We loaded my car the night before moving Nira into the dorms at college. Then I lay in bed all night and stared at the ceiling, listening to Adam's monstrous snores beside me. I knew it would be good for Nira, but the last thing I wanted was for her to leave. To leave me behind in this mess of a home with a neglectful husband and two thankless children. But it wasn't her fault. This was the bed I made for myself and it was me who should suffer for it.

Neither Sarah nor Eric were helpful around the home. They were eleven at the time and content with throwing both clean and dirty clothes on the floor, leaving dishes around the house, and tracking in dirt or snow. They didn't listen to scolding and couldn't care less about punishments.

Sarah started sneaking out at night. Eric was a recluse, content to spend all his time alone in his room. And Adam was Adam—a miserable lump of a man with no desire to do a single thing. I no longer had a companion in my home.

Adam drove Nira to school alone. I couldn't bear the thought of an emotional goodbye in front of an audience so we did it at home. I held Nira for a long time before letting her go to live her life. After they left I sat on the floor in Nira's room and cried. Then I packed up the rest of her things. Sarah was going to take Nira's room, as her current room wasn't much bigger than a small closet. But the real reason I packed up Nira's things was because it was cleansing for me. Years later, Nira informed me it had

79

been hurtful to her. But in my own selfishness, knowing I was trapped in that house, I never thought of how it would affect her for me to pack up her childhood room.

Two months after Nira moved into the dorm I slipped on a patch of ice and broke my right leg. I was put in a cast and on crutches. On the third day of trying to maneuver around the house without any help from anyone I called Nira crying. I knew I shouldn't be bothering her, and that she was getting adjusted to a new place and new friends, but I was an invalid without any assistance.

Nira came home from school one day to me balancing on my crutches in the kitchen in front of an assortment of uncooked food. The kitchen was still the same drab, old-fashioned mess of a room as when we moved in. Adam never followed through with his promise to remodel and I don't know why I was surprised—he never kept his promises. Eric, Sarah, and Adam were all sprawled in front of the television in the living room. Nira tossed her keys and purse on the table. "What are you doing?" she asked.

"Making dinner."

"Why, Mom? Go sit down." She tried to pull me from the counter.

"Mom!" Eric called from the living room.

Nira and I looked at each other, both aware of the horribleness of the situation—the fact that I was a servant in my own home.

"Yes?" I called back.

"Can you bring me a soda?"

Nira's eyes grew wide, her face paled in anger. Red splotches appeared across her chest. Soon there would be smoke coming out of her ears.

"Don't," I said. I didn't want her causing trouble.

She shook her head. "This is ridiculous." She stormed into the living room.

I didn't have to follow her. I could imagine the looks of distaste she received. From my spot in the kitchen, propped up against the counter on my crutches, I could hear everything.

"Are you people kidding me?" Nira raised her voice. "What is your problem?" I doubt this was directed to any one specific person.

"What's your problem?!" Sarah screeched back.

I was unsure if my presence would make things worse or not but I hobbled on my crutches into the living room.

Nira lowered her voice, which was always scarier than her loud voice. "Um, Mom is on crutches. She does not need to be running around waiting on all of you."

"She's fine," Adam said.

I glared at him. I could be in a full body cast and he would still think I was fine enough to wait hand and foot on him.

"What?" he said.

Nira crossed her arms. "If she was fine she wouldn't be in a cast." She turned to face Eric and said, "Is it necessary that she get your drink for you? You can't get up off the couch and do it yourself?"

Eric shrugged. "She was already in the kitchen."

My mouth dropped open, as did Nira's.

"That's totally unacceptable," she said.

"You know you're not in charge, right?" Sarah asked.

Nira took a deep breath. I was afraid she might breathe fire in Sarah's direction. Nira said, "It would be nice if you could all help Mom out a little right now."

Sarah, Eric, and Adam looked at me. Did they need confirmation? Could they not realize that helping me around the house would be beneficial to my well-being? I nodded so they knew I agreed with Nira.

Being the person—the daughter—that she was she packed a bag and came home for three weeks. She borrowed my car to commute to classes but helped me to not lose my head around the house. When she returned to school I was forced to go through Nira withdrawal all over again.

*

After visiting the college I went to Elsa's for help with the application. "I'm not smart enough for this." As soon as I become self-deprecating Elsa tensed.

"I'm not going to help you if that's your attitude," she said.

I was tired of filling out forms and was afraid it was a waste of time—that I wouldn't get accepted anyway. I was too old, too stupid.

"I can see you thinking negative thoughts right now," Elsa said.

I smiled. "Shut up."

Elsa remained serious. "Do you want my help or not?"

"Of course."

"Then stop your complaining and finish these forms," she said and hoisted herself from the couch. She went into the kitchen and called out, "How's your essay going?"

She knew I hated yelling from room to room rather than talking face to face like normal people. Adam was a big fan of the yelling and I rather not carry that over into my new life.

I followed her into the kitchen. "The essay is crap."

Elsa gave me a look that told me to stop pitying myself. She was full of looks. "I'll proof it for you." She opened a bottle of red wine and poured us each a large glass. Mine almost spilled over the rim when I picked it up.

"Thanks," I said before taking a generous gulp.

"What are you writing about?"

"Becoming independent as an old woman."

Elsa laughed. "Well, they always say to write what you know."

We returned to the living room and both sat pretzel style on the couch. Although I was by no means thin I could match Elsa in flexibility.

"How's Ruby?" Elsa asked. It was the first night I was staying over my sister's house since I'd fled to Ruby's in New York City and then got my own apartment. Billy was working late so we had the whole place to ourselves.

"Ruby's been great," I said. I shifted on the couch and unfolded my legs. "She's bent over backwards to make me feel comfortable, as if I haven't felt like a member of her home since we were kids."

"Is she so great she's going to help you get a job?"

"What is that supposed to mean?"

Elsa laughed. "I might be able to help you find something."

"Really?" I couldn't contain my excitement—I sounded like a little girl. A lot of things changed since the last time I was employed and I didn't know where to start.

"I've got my connections," Elsa said. Of course she did. She was an ass-kisser, a social climber. "I know someone at one of the elementary schools. I can get you an interview. And they always want to find people who are pursuing their own education, so going for your masters will be a big plus." Elsa worked for the Department of Education. To be honest, I wasn't sure what the details of her job entailed. She was always going back to school for additional degrees that led to promotions.

Staying in little girl mode I clapped my hands.

"Contain your excitement. First you need to get this application submitted."

I scrunched my face in disgust. "Okay, Mom," I said.

"Speaking of Mom, I told her you went on a date with Rick."

"What?" I rolled my eyes. "Why would you do that?"

"I ran out of things to say and she wouldn't let me get off the phone."

It was hard to yell at Elsa, since I had been in that same position many times. "But did you have to tell her about Rick? Seriously?"

Elsa shrugged. "Like I said, I couldn't think of anything else."

"She was asking when you and Billy are getting married, wasn't she?"

My sister paled a little, looking guilty. It was a look of hers that I was familiar with—it hadn't changed much since we were children. Gabriella, although the one who was consistently guilty, never mastered the look. She was more in favor of going wide-eyed and putting the blame on someone else (usually me).

"Ugh! Yes," Elsa said and offered a little smile.

"I'm going to kill you," I said. "What did you tell her?"

"That the date was miserable."

"I bet she was thrilled."

"Yes, well, she wasn't devastated."

"Mmmhmm." I did a perfect imitation of our mother.

"I told her maybe you married the lesser of two evils."

I burst out laughing. "I'm sure she loved that!"

"All she said was that none of her daughters had any luck with men. I didn't have the heart to tell her she and dad were the reason."

"Maybe you should have."

Elsa shook her head. "You have no soul. Why burden them with the truth this late in their lives?"

"Because they never took responsibility for what they did to us!"

"It wasn't that bad."

She didn't understand. She'd been too young and had me to protect her. I'd had no one. "You don't remember," I said. "It was awful."

"Okay," she said, throwing her arms up in the air in defeat. "Let's get back to your application."

Yes, let's. Better to exhaust myself with the possibilities ahead rather than the traumatization of the past.

Chapter 14

My mother called me before the ambulance. My father was clutching his chest, couldn't speak, yet she called me first. As if I was magical or possessed medical knowledge I didn't know about. I told her to call an ambulance. Despite living only fifteen minutes from the nearest hospital I knew Mother wasn't capable of driving, and told her I would meet them there. I maintained a good fake calm voice—until I got into the car, started driving toward the hospital, and had to call Elsa. I held the cell phone clenched so tightly in my hand that I lost the feeling in my fingers.

"Are you sitting down?" I asked, not wanting to send Elsa racing to the hospital in an ambulance as well.

"What's going on?"

I could hear the tension in her voice.

"Dad's headed to the hospital."

"What happened? Is Mom with him? Where are you?"

"Take deep breaths," I told her, also reminding myself. I didn't need to hyperventilate and drive off the road or into a tree. I thought of Nira and hoped she didn't see the impact coming.

"Yeah, I'm breathing. What's happened?"

"He's having chest pains. Mom went with him in an ambulance."

"Where are you? Are you on your way to the hospital?"

I nodded before remembering she couldn't see me. "Yes, I'm driving there now."

"Well, Jesus, Janie, get off the goddamned phone before you end up in the hospital, too," she said and hung up on me. She was right. I tossed the phone onto the front passenger seat and focused on my driving. Would the world be better off if my father finally died? My memories of him were clouded with hate and disgust, but I could still remember a sliver of his decency from when he interacted with his grandchildren. If only he'd treated Gabriella, Elsa, and me the way he did my children.

I arrived in less than forty minutes. I parked at a slant, forgot to lock the doors, and ran in through the Emergency entrance. There were people everywhere. Bloody, bruised, damaged people. I looked for my mother and father but didn't spot them. Shoving my way through the beat up mass I placed my hand on the welcome desk and stared at the woman scribbling notes in front of me.

"Can I help you?" she asked as she chewed on her pen.

"I'm looking for Howard Freedman. I'm his daughter. He came in an ambulance," I added, trying to be helpful.

"Hold on while I look him up," she said and typed on her keyboard. "He's in the ER, all the way at the end of the hall on the left. There's a waiting room there that the doctor will come talk to you in."

"Thank you," I said and flew down the hall, coat flapping behind me.

The hallway wasn't exceptionally long but I was out of breath when I reached the end. I rested against the wall and tried to bring my breathing back to normal. When I looked up I noticed my mother seated before me, head in hands, shaking.

"Mom?" I sat in the empty seat next to her.

She lifted her head and looked at me with dirty tear streaks running down her face. Her eyes were swollen and her lips quivered. I'd never seen her like that before.

"Did you talk to the doctor? Is it bad?" I couldn't understand why she'd been crying so hard. Why she looked so awful. I guess I expected to see some sort of relief at the possibility of no longer having to deal with my father.

"No. No one will talk to me," she said through sniffles.

I looked around for someone who worked there. A slim nurse sped by, clipboard in hand.

"Excuse me," I called. She kept moving one white clog in front of another so I chased after her. "Nurse?" I took long strides until I was in front of her and could cut her off.

She stopped short. "Yes?"

"My mother brought my father in a little while ago. By ambulance. No one will tell her what's going on."

I swear the nurse almost shrugged. Maybe she saw my expression and thought better of it.

"Name?" she asked.

"Howard Freedman."

"If you just go back to the waiting area I'll have a doctor come speak with you."

"Are you sure?" The fear for my father's life was giving me some vigor. Although I was still unclear as to whether I feared his living or dying more. "If I tell my mother that and no one comes to give us information she might start a scene." Or I might. Either way, we needed to know what the hell was going on.

The nurse nodded. "Someone will be with you shortly."

I didn't believe her, but I headed back to my mother anyway. She was still curled up, still looked half her size.

She stared at me with glassy eyes when I sat beside her.

"A nurse is checking on Dad. She said a doctor will come over soon to tell us the situation."

"Mmmhmm," my mother responded. She rocked back and forth, back and forth.

"If no one comes over I'll walk around and look for someone again, okay?"

"Where's Elsa?" she asked, as if I'd said nothing.

"I don't know. Do you want me to call her?"

She nodded and placed her head in her hands again.

I stepped outside and called my sister. The fresh air was a relief after the nose-clogging hospital smells. "Where are you?" I asked when Elsa answered.

"I'm leaving the house now. Be there in twenty. Any updates?" As she was the perfect daughter I was surprised that she hadn't left yet.

"No, nothing. What's taking you so long?"

"It was supposed to be my day off," Elsa said.

"Ok," I said, still unsure as to why she wasn't hustling her little butt to the hospital. "I should get back in there in case the doctor comes around."

"Okay. Give mom a hug for me?"

"See you soon," I said and hung up. She could give Mother a hug herself in twenty minutes.

I walked back into the hospital. A baby-faced but muscular male doctor was seated with mother, their heads close together in conspiracy. I hurried over.

"Is everything okay?" I asked.

The doctor looked startled. "And you are?"

"This is Janie, my oldest," my mother said. "Where's Elsa?" she asked again.

"She's on her way," I said, exasperated. Didn't it matter that I was already there? Why did she need Elsa?

"I'm the lead doctor on this case. Your father should be okay."

"What's wrong with him?" I asked. I just wanted to know whether my dad was going to make it or not. I wanted to know if mother would get a few years of peace.

"Heart attack. His arteries are ninety-nine percent blocked. But we've got the best doctors working on him."

I sat in a chair on the other side of my mother and held her hand in mine. "How can he be okay with that much blockage?" I asked as I caressed my mother's hand. She might be a miserable old bitch, but she was still my mother.

"He was fortunate to get to the hospital as quickly as he did. He will be brought down to the Cath lab soon for an angioplasty. After we successfully remove the blockage, Mr. Freedman will be moved to the coronary care unit where you will be able to visit him."

The double doors opened to the ER and my father was rushed out on a cot. My mother and I both jumped out of our seats.

"What's going on?" my mother asked.

The doctor smiled. He probably thought it was reassuring, but he looked more like the wolf from Little Red Riding Hood. He needed dental work. "They are taking him to the Cath lab now." He stood and stuck his hand out. My mother shook it. By the look on his face I could tell he was impressed by the power behind her handshake, even if she was a crying mess at the moment.

We waited three hours while the doctors performed the procedures. In that time I chewed off what little nails I had left, Mother drank six cups of coffee, and Elsa arrived at the hospital in rare form. Her hair was unbrushed, her clothes untucked, and the sleep was still in her eyes. I never saw her look like such a mess.

While Elsa and Mother huddled in the corner whispering, nothing new there, I struck up a conversation with the young man sitting next to me.

"What are you reading?" I asked, even though I could clearly see the book was mathematical.

The boy looked at me and smiled. He couldn't have been much younger than Sarah and Eric. "Something boring for school. Who are you here for?"

"My father. He had a heart attack."

"My grandfather also had a heart attack. How old is your dad?"

"In his 80s."

"My grandfather, too. Is it common for their age?"

"I guess everything becomes more common as you get older."

He nodded. "He raised me. I don't have any other family." The smile slipped from his face.

Poor kid. I might not be the biggest fan of my family but at least I had one.

"I'm sorry to hear that. What have the doctors said?"

"It doesn't look good. This is his third heart attack." He tucked one leg under him. "I don't know what I'll do without him."

I couldn't even imagine my own children talking about their grandfather that way. I doubted they would even notice he was gone from our lives, when the time came. When they were little, Nira spent a lot of time with my parents. Sometimes it seemed as if they saved their love for me to give to her.

"I'm sure you have good friends that will help you through this?" I asked, not sure at all.

His face brightened a bit. "I do. I have a wonderful girlfriend. Pop-pop loves her, too."

I smiled. It felt strange to turn my mouth in an upward direction. "Then she must be a very special person."

We were interrupted by a doctor wanting to give the boy an update. The doctor spoke in a hushed tone and led the boy from the room. He didn't look back.

Several minutes later my father's doctor entered the waiting room and my mother, sister, and I stood. "Everything looks good. We did end up having to insert a stent into one of the heart's arteries. I've prescribed an anti-clotting medication that he will need to take for at least twelve months. Will you be able to assist in that?" he asked my mother. She had started to return to normal while we waited for my father to come out of the Cath lab. I'm not sure if it was because she decided to accept what was happening around her, but I was glad she'd snapped out of it. Seeing her so vulnerable was unnerving.

"Of course I can handle giving my husband his medication," my mother replied. Yes, she was definitely back to normal.

"Good, good," the doctor said. He stood and stretched. "We'll be able to release him in about five days."

"Thank you," my mother said, without a hint of actual gratitude.

"You should get some rest," Elsa said to her. "And we should look into rehab."

"No, no rehab. I'll take care of your father," my mother said.

"Can we see him now?" I asked, ignoring her.

The doctor nodded. "A nurse can bring you down to his room in the coronary care unit."

He grabbed a nurse who was passing by and we followed her down several white, shiny halls and a cramped elevator before arriving at my father's room. Elsa and my mother rushed inside while I remained, reluctant, at the door.

My father was already frail, weak. I was afraid to see what he would look like lying in a hospital bed. But I didn't have a choice so I put one foot in front of the other and joined my mother and sister by his side. He looked worse than I expected. His lips were chapped and covered with dried blood, his skin the color of damp clay. He had seen better days.

My mother held his left hand, my sister his right. I sat in a chair in the corner and resumed my regular, quiet role. I watched my mother whisper into my father's ear, saw him offer a weak smile. It was if they were the only two in the room. It was amazing and disgusting at the same time. I needed to accept that while I was moving on with my own life, my mother would remain where she was in hers.

Chapter 15

Dear Janie,

Congratulations on being accepted to the class of 2015! I am pleased to welcome you to the Master's Program in Special Education. Please accept my personal congratulations for your outstanding achievement.

I was so excited the letter was shaking in my hand. I never thought I would actually get accepted. I never thought I would really be moving on with my life. That I would have a life. I could feel the smile stretch across my face—so wide it hurt. But it was a good hurt.

Elsa was already on her way over and it was all I could do to keep from jumping out of my skin. I walked circles around the apartment. Mo followed, Maxie sat and watched. I ate a giant chocolate bar and drank half a bottle of wine before Elsa let herself into the apartment—she had the only spare key. I was with the dogs, panting as we waited forever for her to turn the key and push the door open. When Elsa finally stepped inside she took one look at me and laughed.

"I got in!" I yelled a little too loud. Maxie ran behind the couch.

"What?"

I grabbed the acceptance letter off the coffee table and waved it in Elsa's face. "I'm going to graduate school!"

"Wahoo!" Elsa wrapped her small arms around me. "I'm so happy for you."

"You're happy?" I laughed. "I'd dance if I wasn't so coordination-challenged."

"Please don't. You'll only hurt yourself."

I punched her in the arm. "I want to celebrate. What can we do?"

"Do you want to go out?"

Normally, that would've been the dumbest question in the world. "Yes, please."

"Ok," she said. "Let's go out for a drink. Maybe some appetizers?"

"Perfect." I grabbed my coat from the front closet.

We walked a few blocks to a lively dive bar many people didn't know about. Jimmy's Corner was old and small, as was most of its clientele. Elsa and I liked it because we were the youngest, hottest babes there.

We sat at the bar and ordered girly drinks. The bartender, a woman somewhere in her seventies with fake breasts spilling out of a tank top, seemed underwhelmed by my excitement at acceptance to graduate school.

The handsome man a few stools down was leaning just a few inches toward us with a lopsided grin on his face. I pointed him out to Elsa as I sipped on my calorie-riddled mudslide.

"He's cute," Elsa stated the obvious.

His hair was light brown and he was younger than us. I wasn't sure by how much. I was having trouble keeping my eyes off him, and every time I tried to nonchalantly take a glance over Elsa's shoulder the stranger and I made eye contact.

I felt the heat in my cheeks.

"What's up?" Elsa asked, always the first to notice anything.

"I don't know. I keep looking at that man. I'm embarrassing."

"Go talk to him."

"What? Don't be crazy. No. Maybe after another drink."

I summoned the bartender and ordered a Long Island Iced Tea. That ought to do the trick.

"A long island?" Elsa asked and raised an eyebrow.

"Do you want me to be socially lubricated or not?"

She shrugged. "How much of a fool do you want to make of yourself?"

I thought about it. "Medium?"

We both laughed. Out of the corner of my eye I noticed a small smirk on the face of the handsome man. I wondered how much he had heard and again my face felt hot.

I lowered my voice. "Do you think he can hear us?"

"Possibly. How's the liquid courage feeling?"

I evaluated myself. I felt loose. "Good. But I have no idea how to approach him."

Elsa glared at me. "You get off your butt, walk over there, and bat your big eyes at him." Rick had often referred to them, as positively as possible, as my big cow eyes.

"Fine," I said and slid off the stool. I gulped down my drink before taking an awkward step forward. My feet looked unsure as I stared at the ground.

"Did you drop something?"

I looked up and the handsome man was standing before me. I had barely made it two feet from where Elsa and I were seated.

Too startled to speak, I just opened and closed my mouth repeatedly.

"Can I buy you a drink?" he asked.

One drink quickly led to two and then we were talking about music, movies, and books. We never spoke about family. I never had to bring up the sordid topic of divorce. And before I knew it Elsa was tapping on my back.

"I'm going to head out," she said.

"Oh, okay." I slung my purse over my shoulder.

Elsa shook her head. "Take a cab," she said and moved her eyes toward the man that had occupied most of my time that evening.

"Unless you don't want to have another drink with me?" the man directed to me.

Elsa disappeared before I had a chance to make my own decision.

"One more drink," I agreed.

I had one final drink. Then I went home with a stranger for the first time.

*

Against my better judgment, I agreed to meet my mother for lunch when she came into the city to shop one day. We kept it low-key and met at a Jewish deli near my apartment. I knew she would appreciate the location because they served a lot of her favorite things: babka (pastry-like loaf), brisket (cut of beef), and gefilte fish (stuffed fish). Some things I hated while growing up and some I loved.

I arrived first. Mother always had us show up late for events while growing up and I didn't expect today to be any different. When she finally entered the deli I couldn't help but notice she seemed smaller, as if she had shrunk. Despite her smaller stature, she stood up straight and did something I hadn't seen in years. She smiled.

I stood and gave her a hug when she approached the small round table where I was seated. "You look good," I said. I was happy for her.

"I've been getting more sleep," she replied. "Did you already order?"

"No, I was waiting for you."

We walked to the counter together, happy mother happy daughter, and each ordered brisket with a piece of chocolate babka for dessert.

Situated back at the table we waited for the counter person to bring over our food.

"How are things?" I asked.

"Good. I've been spending more time with the girls."

The girls were a group of women that my mother played bridge with. Before father fell ill mother played on a weekly basis. But, as many women have done in the past and will continue to do in the future, she pushed her own life and needs aside to care for an ungrateful man.

"They let me win for a while," she added. "But I told them I wanted none of that. So now I'm losing again." Mother chuckled. The sound was foreign and unfamiliar.

"How's dad?" I had to ask. In spite of everything, he was still my father. Even if I had trouble visiting lately. Mother hired a nurse to help at home after father ended up in the hospital. Seeing him in that condition and watching a stranger take care of him in his own home was too much for me. I visited once and hadn't been back since.

The counter person came over and gently placed our plates in front of us. I nodded thanks.

"The same," she said and struggled to cut through a fatty piece of brisket.

I didn't know if that meant bitter and angry or disabled and demented.

"Better or worse than at the hospital?" I asked and carved into my own slice of beef.

Mother put her fork down and dabbed at her mouth with a napkin. "Since you asked," she said and sighed. "He is worse. I have decided to put him in hospice care."

"Really?" I chewed the fibrous meat thoroughly. Was she admitting that she couldn't do it on her own anymore, even with the help of a nurse? She had never admitted defeat before.

"It's not what I want. But it is for the best. The doctor's say so, anyway."

Now she was listening to the advice of doctors?

"It will also cost less than the nurse at home. I would like to preserve some of your and Elsa's inheritance, if I can."

"I think it's a great idea, Mom."

"I know. But it has been just him and me for so many years."

"You'll be fine," I said. "Just think of all the extra time you'll have to spend with the girls. Maybe you'll even find a boyfriend."

She nearly spit out her food. "Janie!"

I smiled until she smiled back.

*

For the first time in my life I wasn't nervous. Elsa had set up a job interview for me as a special education aide in a second grade classroom. I went into the interview full of myself and my skills. I kept repeating what Elsa had said, "They don't care that you haven't been in a classroom for thirty years—you ran your own classroom at home with three children." She never spoke truer words.

Fifteen minutes into the interview I was offered the job. I walked out with my head held high. I could see more than I used to, when I would slouch and hang my head low. I was getting more and more used to this new confidence, and it was starting to show. Why else would I be offered a job so quickly? Things were going so well that it was obvious I should have left Adam decades earlier. I had finally grown tired of playing the victim, of blaming others for decisions I was too weak to make. Who knew where my life would go now? How much better it could still be?

Chapter 16

I loved my new apartment. I loved the decorating, the fancy doorman, and even knowing that if I had to clean a toilet it was my own shit I'd be cleaning. But, most of all, I loved my solitude. Maxie and Mo didn't seem to miss our old home, either.

To contrast all the bright shininess of the apartment I brought in lots of my two favorite colors—black and red. I purchased red velvet drapes, a black suede couch, and a matching black furniture set that glowed with a dull sheen. I littered dried roses throughout the apartment. It was soothing, breathtaking. And it was all mine.

I didn't tell many people where I was living. I just wasn't ready yet. So when the doorbell rang I was genuinely confused as to who it could be.

"Hello?" I asked as I pushed the "Talk" button over the intercom.

"Janie, it's Rick."

I was overwhelmed by thoughts of Why? and Who invited you? "Hi... What are you doing here?" I asked.

"I really need to talk. Can you buzz me in?"

Without hesitation, I hit the button to let him inside. A few minutes later, longer than it took most people, he was at my door.

He looked like raw meat. His face was red, blue, and black; his left eye sealed shut. His right arm was in a sling and he walked with a limp.

"What the hell happened?" I moved aside so he could hobble into my apartment.

He collapsed onto the beautiful black couch. "Adam happened."

I shook my head. "Hold on," I said. "Before you start, do you want something to drink?"

"Yes. Something strong."

I briskly walked to the kitchen and looked through my liquor cabinet. I had been trying to drink less hard alcohol since Adam and I split, since Adam seemed like the reason I drank anyway. But tucked in the back of the cabinet, behind the wines and spritzers that I now drank, was a bottle of vodka Elsa had given me. I poured two glasses, neat, and walked back into the living room.

Rick eagerly took the glass as I sat next to him on the couch.

"I'm so sorry," I said. I didn't know what else to say so I offered him an extra cushiony pillow.

He shook his head and put his glass down on the coffee table. "Definitely not your fault." He took the pillow and propped himself up. "But that ex of yours is certifiable."

I chuckled without humor. "I know. Huge reason why I left."

"Well, I guess he didn't believe it when you said nothing is going on between us."

I nodded. "So what happened?"

"He showed up at my office. I was working late, again. I don't know where the night doorman was and I had no secretary on duty to run interference. Adam walked right on in. I was pretty shocked to see him. He didn't even try to explain, or give me a chance to explain. He immediately punched me in the face." Rick touched his left eye gingerly, probably thinking about the damage that had been done to his near perfect good looks. I actually thought the bruises added character. "He's a big guy, Janie."

"Yeah, I know."

"You sure he never got more physical than you told me?"

"I'm sure. He really was more bark than bite."

"Yeah, well, not with me. He basically twisted my arm and leg in ways I never imagined possible. After I went to the ER and filed a police report, I thought it would be a good idea to take a cab here and let you know what happened. I didn't think this was the kind of story I should deliver over the phone."

I offered a weak smile. "Probably not."

"I imagine the police are probably out looking for Adam right now."

"Hopefully they find him?"

"Is that a question?" Rick asked, his eyes wide.

"No," I answered slowly. "But I just can't help feeling responsible for all of this."

"It's not your fault, Janie. The man is a lunatic. I've worked with lots of men like him. It has nothing to do with you." He took a big swig of his drink. And then another. Before long he was slurring his words. "Not yer fault at all. Yer a bootiful woman." He put his hand on my knee.

I moved his hand away and opened my mouth to chastise him. Before I could say anything there was another buzz, another unexpected visitor.

Rick and I both froze, staring at each other.

"No way," Rick said and shook his head.

I lifted myself off the couch, dead weight, and walked as if moving through water to get to the buzzer.

Closing my eyes, I pressed on the buzzer. "Who is it?"

"Janie," Adam said, "Let me in."

I looked at Rick. He shook his head and sighed.

"What do I do?" I asked.

"Well, don't let him in!"

"Please go away," I said into the intercom.

"We need to talk."

"That's what a restraining order is all about, Adam. You shouldn't even be here."

"Just let me come up to talk to you."

"It's not happening. You need to leave or I'm calling the police." I don't know why I even continued to keep my finger moving from "Talk" to "Listen". Why wasn't there an "Ignore"?

"I'm staying right here until you come down."

"We have nothing to talk about. Our marriage is over."

His breathing got louder, deeper. He sounded in pain. "I just want to talk," he said, sounding like a small child.

"Adam." I, too, sounded young. Pleading. "Just go away." I grew stronger every day, but the sound of his voice still ripped me apart.

"Are you coming down?" he asked.

I'd had enough. I released the "Listen" button and backed away.

"You should call the police now," Rick said. "They're looking for him anyway."

My cell phone found its way into my hand and I dialed the local sheriff's number, pinned to the corkboard on the wall next to the yellow pages. And I proceeded to have my husband of over three decades arrested. There was going to be no more breaking the rules, breaking the restraining order, or breaking Rick's face. No more walking all over me. No more making me feel bad for doing what's best for me. I hoped Adam enjoyed his time in jail.

Chapter 17: One Year Later

I had far too many books. The dogs and I could barely get through the maze in my apartment to reach our various destinations. Needless to say, I completely threw myself into grad school. I absorbed everything. I was a sea sponge, attaching myself to any piece of knowledge I could find.

I did well, too. I impressed myself. Some of my professors were younger than me, but even they had knowledge to share. I held a study group at my apartment weekly, filled with like-minded individuals wanting to further themselves. Nothing like the way I used to spend my evenings.

Sarah came by the apartment only once. She put back on some of the weight she shed and looked healthy. She looked so much like Nira it hurt. But it hurt most that she didn't come to see me more often. She was on a regular schedule for visiting Adam.

Eric rarely visited, but at least introduced me to his fiancé. She was tanned and toned, just like him. He told me they would have a small wedding and I wouldn't be invited. Even as my heart broke a little more, something I accepted would never stop happening, I wasn't surprised.

Rick tried to get me to go on another date with him. I didn't understand how he thought I'd enjoyed the first one, although I had to give him credit for continuing to try. Even the life-long dream of sleeping with him wasn't enough to motivate me to go on another date. Sometimes the fantasy was simply better than the reality.

Father didn't last much longer after he went into hospice. At that point I had lost a sister, a daughter, and a father. Now I just wanted to lose the husband. And the big day had finally come. Divorce Day. When the mail arrived I wasn't sure it would be there. The piece of paper that ended another life, another me. Stamped with the judge's seal of approval, the final divorce decree said it all. I was finally done with Adam.

Adam was in prison, anyway. The crazy bastard couldn't get away with anything anymore. That's what happens when you commit forgery, violate restraining orders, and beat someone up. When the charges piled up and Adam was arrested, he couldn't make bail. Thomas had snorted all his money. I almost felt bad for Adam, but not quite. There were no issues with the preliminary conference for our divorce because he had nothing left to fight for. Adam received a total of thirteen years of jail time: one year for breaking the restraining order, five years for forgery in the first degree, and seven years for second-degree assault against Rick. It would be strange to have him finally and completely gone from my life, as if our relationship never happened. But it would also be wonderful.

CPSIA information can be obtained
at www.ICGtesting.com
Printed in the USA
LVHW111602300421
686093LV00005B/480